THE MEANI

Detective John Gammon Series Three
Book Five

Book Five from Series Three of the John Gammon Peak District Detective series set in the beautiful Peak District.

A big thank you to Martyn Wright for yet again producing a fabulous cover for the book. Again great work from Gill Barr-Colbeck in getting this sorted. A big thank you Gill.

I hope you enjoy the book as much as I did writing it. If you did please take a look at my web-site **www.colingaltrey.co.uk**

THE MEANING STONES

Christmas is a special time in Britain and there isn't any where more stunning to spend Christmas than in the beautiful Peak District of Derbyshire, renowned for its natural beauty.

When acting DCI John Gammon stumbles on a case of such gruesome detail it sends the community at this special time into a concern that not only were they in real danger, but the industry of tourism that most of the local businesses rely on was being damaged.

Gammon and his team knew they had to work fast to get closure because of the catastrophic effect a serial killer could

Detective John Gammon Series Three
Book Five

have on their community and their lively-

hoods. The pressure was on.

THE MEANING STONES

Contents

Detective John Gammon Series Three
Book Five

CHAPTER ONE

The shock John felt when Fleur told him
about Anouska and the baby was beyond
comprehension. John poured himself a
very large Jameson's and sat at the kitchen
table. The truth was he was no longer the
father of Anka Emily; but the big shock
was what Fleur told him. His best friend
Steve Lineman was the father. They had
his DNA on record because of his recent
stay in jail.

Now he had to console himself that as
far as Saron knew he hadn't lied that night
when she asked him if he had a baby,

THE MEANING STONES

because it wasn't his. Did Anouska know that? Was Steve a one night stand or something more? And finally did he tell Steve now after all this trouble Anouska had caused, and for what he thought?

John Gammon was about to experience a killer with no scruples, no fear and certainly no heart. This person or persons were beyond redemption.

It was 9.20am and Gammon was playing catch up with his pet hate, paperwork. This was the day he would never forget. The phone rang it was Magic on the front desk.

Detective John Gammon Series Three
Book Five

"Sir, I have a very distraught gentleman who wants to see you."

"Ok I'll be down."

At first Gammon thought the man had been in an accident, he was covered in blood.

"DCI Gammon, and you are?"

"Welbeck Styler," the man said, his voice quivering.

"How can I help you, Mr Styler?"

The man started to cry.

"Magic, get Mr Styler a drink. "We will be in room one."

Gammon sat the man down, he was so distraught. Magic placed a glass of water on

THE MEANING STONES

the table and the man struggled to lift the glass to his mouth he was shaking so badly.

"Right Mr Styler, in your own time explain to me what the problem is."

"I am a professional wildlife and landscape photographer, so I was out at sunrise to get some shots of Magpie Mine. It's such a fabulous thing to photograph, if you get the light right, and quite often you will see a badger or a fox on its way home after a night feeding somewhere."

"I headed to the tall chimney and next to it, is what would have been a coal store and a stone."

"A stone? What do you mean a stone?"

"You know, like you see at the side of the road, that might say Bixton to London a hundred and thirty miles."

"Ok, so what was significant about the stone?"

"Well nothing at first. I didn't notice because the door was unusually swung open on the coal store. I had never seen the door open before, so I was inquisitive. As I got closer, I could see the lock had been broken."

Styler then became upset again.

"Take your time, Mr Styler."

Styler composed himself again.

THE MEANING STONES

"I looked inside, but it was empty. Either whatever had been in there had been removed, or kids had forced the door. I shut the door and that's when I got the shock. There was a man, I would say in his fifties, quite a portly chap, balding with a grey moustache. Something had removed his eyes and replaced them with a pair of dice and sat him against the stone using it like a chair back."

"Just a moment Mr Styler."

Gammon went out and told Magic to get Wally and a team up to Magpie Mine.

"So this man, I am assuming, was dead when you found him?"

"Yes, he was covered in blood, that's
how I ended up in this mess. It was
dreadful, Mr Gammon."

"I'm sure it was, just let me take some
details if you don't mind?"

"It got worse, Mr Gammon. I did try to
help the poor man, but he was dead and
that's when I saw one if his eyes
positioned so that it was looking at him on
top of the stone."

"So, your full name is?"

"Welbeck Styler. I live at The Old
Creamery in Pritwich. I work as a
freelance photographer for wildlife
magazines."

THE MEANING STONES

"Are you married, Mr Styler?"

"Yes, to Amy, she is a local girl. Amy Saunders was her maiden name."

"Blimey, yes, I do know Amy. She will be the same age as me. I heard she had gone to live in Ireland."

"Yes, that was Amy's hippy phase, as she calls it. She went to Ireland to find herself and found me. I'm afraid."

"Didn't Meredith Saunders live at the Creamery?"

"Yes, she was Amy's grandma, she left the house to her when she passed away."

"Blimey, small world Mr Styler, give Amy my best."

"I will Mr Gammon. Do you need anything else from me?"

"Not at the moment, but I know where you are if we need to chat some more."

Styler left and Gammon set off for Magpie Mine. The Mine stood on the outskirts of a small rural village called Shealdon. It had a small village pub, The Broken Egg, so called because during the first World War when rationing was at its peak, the then landlord kept hens. This by default gave him plentiful eggs and he would give them to the locals so they could bake etc. But one night a government man was seen doing a house

THE MEANING STONES

to house search for illegal keeping of animals that could produce food. The landlord panicked. He rushed outside and began throwing the eggs over the wall. In all the government man found six hundred eggs, and the hens were confiscated, and the man fined. He was lucky not to be sent to prison

At the time of the First World War the pub was called the Black Bull, but it shut. Many years later after a refurb it re-opened and a local man bought it. He called it The Broken Egg because of the story and the locals naming it the Broken

Egg after the event with the government man.

The mine had been a source of employment for many of the local men until it finally closed in 1958. It hadn't produced much lead for the last eight years before closure. It had now become listed and was a photographer's dream at dusk or dawn with the tall Cornish type chimney creating an unsurpassed backdrop.

Gammon loved the place and had often walked to it since he had been back in the Peak District. To have a murder here somewhat sullied his thoughts on the

THE MEANING STONES

place. Gammon could see Wally's tent and DS Bass, DI Lee and DI smarty standing near the tent.

"Right, what we got?"

"Not a lot Sir, there is nobody up here. We have had a look round."

"Ok, let me speak with Wally, DI Lee."

"What we got, Wally?"

"A particularly nasty one here, John. The man has been well cut up, his eyes removed and replaced with two dice."

Gammon took one look and almost vomited, it was that sick.

"Ok mate, tomorrow at 9.00am?"

"I will do my best as always, John."

"Come on Dave, I need a drink."

"Where we going?"

"Let's go and have a chat with the locals in the Broken Egg."

Gammon drove them down to Shealdon village and round the back of the pub to the gravelled car park.

It was only 12.30pm but it was still quite busy for a week day.

"What real ales have you got?"

"How strong do you want it, handsome?" said the landlady.

"About a 4.2 would be good."

"Ok duck, we have Barmaids Apron, Sluice Gate and Drooper's Brew."

THE MEANING STONES

That made Dave Smarty smile.

"Two of them, shall we Dave?"

"Sound's good to me, mate."

The landlady came back with the beer.

"Six pounds eighty please, ma duck."

John handed her seven pounds and told her to put the change in the air ambulance box.

"Hey, what a cracking pub, John. Do you come here often?"

"No, first time I have been, but heard the food was great."

They both ordered a ploughman's and sat talking about the gruesome find at Magpie Mine.

Detective John Gammon Series Three
Book Five

"What do you reckon, Dave? What is the significance of the dice replacing the eyes?"

"I don't know John, if I didn't know better, I would say it's some kind of gangland killing."

"Don't rule it out Dave, if the guy was on the run for some kind of gambling debt that could be the answer."

That's what Gammon liked about DI Smarty, he was Smarty by name and Smarty by nature he thought.

"Did you read what was on the stone, Dave?"

THE MEANING STONES

"No, Wally gets a bit precious about going on his white tent."

"It was a stone to commemorate the death of five men from Shealdon lost to the First World War."

"Is that something they do up here?"

"Generally all villages have monuments, but in Derbyshire it's quite unique, they often put up stone monuments to different things, and quite often they have a poem written on them."

With the food consumed and the beer drank they headed to the station. On the way Gammon had his friend Steve on his mind. So has soon as he got back in his office he rang him to see if he could meet him that night.

"Could do mate, got a lot to tell you."

Not as much as me thought Gammon.

They agreed to meet at the Sycamore in Pritwich. It had been a bit of time since John had seen Rita and Tony. As he drove to Pritwich that night he wasn't sure he was doing the right thing. Did he let sleeping dogs lie? Let Anouska think he didn't know and carry on paying. The child would never know, but then if it came out, he was sure that would be the end of his and Steve's friendship.

THE MEANING STONES

John walked in and as usual Tony and Rita were pleased to see him.

"Pleased you came in John. Hopefully we will see more of you soon, we have decided to come out of the pub."

"Really, why? It does so well."

"That's part of the problem, John. We have no time to ourselves, so we decided to call it a day. We will be able to go on things with the gang again."

"Oh good, who is taking it?"

"The brewery hasn't said yet, but we have given them three month's notice."

"Pour John a pint of Unicorn on the house, Tony."

"Coming right up mate."

Steve walked in looking really pleased with himself.

"Blimey, good to see you so happy Steve, and out with your mate."

"Yes, all's good in Lineman world, Rita."

"You better get Steve a beer on the house."

Rita explained to Steve that they were leaving. The bar started to fill up so John and Steve sat in the window.

"So mate what you dragged your mate away for?"

"It's a bit difficult, Steve."

THE MEANING STONES

"What is, John?"

"Remember Anouska?"

"Bloody hell John, can't forget her and her body, and of course the aggro caused on your wedding day, mate."

"Well from that she said she was pregnant, and she had a baby called Anka Emily. That's what's wrong Steve. I had a DNA test done, and get ready for this, you are the father."

Steve's face went white.

"That's not possible."

"It's true mate. Your DNA is on the police database and it came up as a match."

"Bloody hell mate, I'm sorry, it was just a one-off."

"Steve, it's not a problem, if anything it's helped me with Saron."

"Well that's second bit of good news today, John."

"Why?"

"Imogen is filing for divorce."

"What?"

"I know it was such a mistake mate. I fell for her on the rebound. I wasn't over Jo, and guess I never will be, but I am going to be free to ask India out."

"But that's Jo's sister."

"I know, and her twin."

THE MEANING STONES

"Don't you think that's a bit weird, Steve?"

"Come on, you would ask her out if you got chance?"

Now did John tell him he had already slept with India? It was probably his best chance, but his mate seemed so happy and he didn't want to spoil that.

"Where does Anouska live, John?"

"A place called Gronk in Latvia."

"Well I best go and see my little girl, and get something arranged. I am assuming you have stopped paying Anouska for the child?"

"Not yet mate, but I will now."

"Ok that's fair John, and thanks for being honest with me. If I ever marry India, you will be my best man again."

More bloody pressure John thought. But his thoughts were on winning Saron back again now he had that monkey off his back.

They had a few more drinks and then called it a night. Steve said he wanted to get back. He had moved back in with Tracey Rodgers, Jo's other sister, in the gate house which he owned anyway. John asked if Tracey knew about India.

"Not yet mate. We said we would tell her together at the weekend."

THE MEANING STONES

"Good luck mate."

It was now almost 11.00pm.

"Shall we make our way, John?"

"Yes, I'm ready."

"Goodnight Tony, tell Rita we will see her soon, mate."

"Ok lads, see you both soon."

The following day John drove into work not knowing that one of his officers was in a serious way.

"Morning, Magic," Gammon said as he strode purposefully into the station.

"Morning Sir, DS Bass is waiting for you. Sir, I'm afraid it's not great news."

"Where is she?"

"She is sat in your office, Sir."

Gammon climbed the stairs and grabbed a coffee before entering his office. DS Bass was sitting crying.

"Whatever is a matter, Kate?"

She struggled at first, but then blurted out that DI Kiernan was in hospital, and it was touch and go.

"What, I don't understand. Has he had a car accident?"

"No Sir, he was picked up by a driver on the Bixton Road in the early hours of this morning, he had been beaten quite severely. The man, a Mr Croker, stopped and got him in his car and took him straight to Bixton. I just took the call and didn't know what to do."

"Tell the rest of the team and Wally we will meet in the Incident room at 1.30 pm today, please Magic."

"Ok Kate, come on let's get over there."

Gammon and Bass headed for the hospital. At reception Gammon showed his warrant card, and was told they were operating on Kiernan at that very moment. She told Gammon to go to Oker ward and wait there. She said the man that brought him in was also waiting.

The nurse on the ward showed Gammon and Bass to a seat next to the gentleman that brought DI Kiernan in. Gammon showed him his warrant card.

"Mr Croker, I'm DCI Gammon and this is DS Bass. I believe you brought DI Kiernan into hospital."

Croker was about fifty eight Gammon thought. He had a dark blue bib and brace and what looked like safety shoes. He had a lot of what looked like cement dust in his hair and on his clothes.

"I would like to ask you a few questions while we wait. Could you tell me your name please?"

THE MEANING STONES

"Sydney Arthur Croker."

"Would you mind if I called you Syd?"

"No, everybody else does."

"So you found DI Kiernan? Where exactly?"

"Just passed the Jug Hare."

"That's close to Obney Cement Works, isn't it?"

"Yes, I work nights."

"So you found DI Kiernan at what time exactly?"

"It was 6.30am. I had just finished my shift at the cement works, and was driving home when I saw this figure staggering in the middle of the road. I assumed he was drunk, and must have been in the Jug on a late session. When I got closer, he fell down so I stopped the car. He was in a terrible state. I managed to get him into the back seat and I brought him straight here. They told me they found his warrant card, so I phoned Bixton station. I decided to stay when they said they were operating on the lad."

"That is very good of you, Syd."

"It's not a problem, I have got kids of my own."

"Listen, we will be staying so if you want to get off give DS Bass your address and phone number."

THE MEANING STONES

"Ok, if you don't mind, it's been a long night."

Croker left, and Gammon rang the station to let them know what had happened

Almost four hours lapsed when the surgeon came out.

"DCI Gammon, come into my office please."

Gammon and Bass followed the surgeon.

"Please take a seat. I'm the surgeon that just operated on Mr Kiernan. He fought gallantly, but I'm afraid his body could not take anymore and we lost him. He died from multiple blows to the head, face and torso. I am very sorry we did our very best, Mr Gammon," and he shook John's hand.

Gammon was shocked. Bass had tears rolling down her cheeks.

"Come on Kate, we best get back. There is nothing we can do here."

They thanked the surgeon then left. On the way back Gammon asked Kate where Kiernan was living and if he had a girlfriend? Kate Bass seemed a little sheepish.

"Sir, we were seeing each other."

THE MEANING STONES

Gammon could hardly be judgemental with his history he thought.

"Oh ok, how long?"

"Only about five weeks."

"Did you see him last night?"

"Yes and we argued."

"What about, Kate?"

"He said he had a theory on the murder at Magpie Mine. He had been restless all night."

"So, did he say what it was?"

"No. This morning I woke at 3.17am by my bedside clock and Danny wasn't in bed, in fact he wasn't in the house. I frantically called his mobile. He answered but was quite sharp."

"What do you mean?"

"He said he was staking out somebody and I wasn't to call."

"Did he say where?"

"No he hung up. Looking back maybe he hadn't got over his girlfriend when we started seeing each other. Possibly it wasn't very professional of me to see a higher ranking officer."

"Kate, don't beat yourself up, none of us can help feelings."

THE MEANING STONES

"Oh, I'm sorry, I wasn't being judgemental. I…," and she stuttered. "I was just explaining what happened to me."

"Don't worry, move on. Let's concentrate on what happened to DI Kiernan."

Back at the station Gammon called Lee and Smarty into his office.

"How well did you know Danny Kiernan?"

"He was a bubbly character, but very focused on moving up the ranks. I could see that could aggravate some of the more seasoned cops."

They both agreed they liked Danny.

Detective John Gammon Series Three
Book Five

"This case he was working on, had he told you two anything about it?"

"No, like I said he wanted the glory himself, to get him up the ladder."

"Ok Peter, I think I get the picture. Thanks lads, let's get down to the incident room and hear what Wally has for us."

Everybody had assembled.

"Before we go any further, we lost DI Kiernan last night. He was badly beaten and died from his injuries. A source close to him said they believed he had a hunch on the Magpie Mine murder, so he was staking that out."

THE MEANING STONES

Gammon didn't want Kate feeling her relationship with Danny was on trial.

"It is possible that either Danny Kiernan uncovered something, or disturbed the killer, either way there is a fair chance that was the case."

"Ok Wally, what have got on the murder victim?"

"He was a white male, fifty four years old. From his dental records his name was Anthony Smidge. He worked as a supervisor at Obney Cement Works, the same place as the guy who found DI Kiernan wandering on the road."

Detective John Gammon Series Three
Book Five

Gammon put all this information on the incident board.

"He was suffocated, then badly beaten before his eyes were gouged out. There is a distinct possibility his eyes were removed while he was in a semi - conscious state. From everything we found at the site, one of Mr Smidges eyes had been taken. We can only assume as some kind of macabre trophy by the killer."

"Right, usual stuff, door to door knocking in the area. See if the owners of the Jug Hare heard or saw anything with regard to DI Kiernan. On that note I have asked his original police force to inform

THE MEANING STONES

Danny's next of kin. I will know more about any funeral arrangements sometime this week. Do we have an address for Anthony Smidge?"

"Yes, it's number 3, Oker Flats, Dilley Dale."

"Ok Carl, take a look at his bank accounts etc."

"Smarty and Lee, you sort out the house to house please."

"DS Bass, I have a job for you."

Gammon had DS Bass looking at known criminals living in the Peak District that had any involvement with Casinos.

His train of thought was something to do with the dice.

He had the unenviable task of going to see Mrs Smidge. Oker Flats had been built on some original council yard. As kids, John and his brother Adam used to go playing cowboys and Indians with Dilley Dale lads in the yard. There were big grit heaps and old buildings they could hide in.

The flats had been built under much protest. The locals felt like they were becoming part of Micklock because of all the building work which was now eating up Green Belt land under new Government legislation. The flats weren't

THE MEANING STONES

particularly well built, and they now harboured just about anybody who had been the fear of the Dilley Dale residents all those years ago.

Gammon found number three Oker Flats and knocked on the door. To his surprise the door wasn't properly shut.

He shouted, "Hello, police, is anybody home?"

There was no answer, so he made his way inside the flat. It had been ransacked. Chairs were upside down and drawers hanging out of cupboards. He quickly phoned the station and told Magic to get Wally and his team down to Dilley Dale.

Detective John Gammon Series Three
Book Five

"Tell DS Yap to come down also."

John came back outside as he didn't want to contaminate the crime scene. While he stood waiting an old lady came past carrying her shopping.

"Tha wunna find old Smidgey in today. They found him bloody dead up at mine tha knows. Who are you anyway?"

Gammon showed her his warrant card.

"Did you know Mr Smidge?"

"Tony were a bloke as kept his self to his self, like other beggars should do as live here."

"Was he married?"

THE MEANING STONES

"No, he were from London originally but came ta flats about six year gone. He worked at cement works. Only know that because bloody washing machines were always clogging up with cement dust off his clothing, and Carol warden were always moaning about it. Well its non-fair to rest on us, is it?"

Gammon saw Wally coming on the walk-way so he made his excuse.

"Oh, by the way how did you know he was murdered?"

"It were on Carol Sky thingy-me-jig that her watches all time."

"Oh ok."

Detective John Gammon Series Three
Book Five

"What we got, John?"

"Something not ringing true here, Wally. The flat has had a right going over. Just picking up bits from that woman I don't think he was from round these parts. See if you can see any clues mate, and let me know."

"DS Yap, do a door to door see if anybody saw anything suspicious, you know, anybody hanging round this flat."

Gammon left them with it and said he would like the results for a meeting around 9.00am tomorrow. Wally rolled his eyes, same old story blood from a stone he thought.

THE MEANING STONES

Late afternoon Kate came back.

"There are three would you believe.
Jack Gibbs, he used to be a croupier in
London and was caught fiddling the black
jack tables. He lives in Ackbourne. Then I
got a Bob Bloom. He actually owned a
casino with his partner, Harbey Clayton, in
the Peak District. They retired but they
fiddled their tax and were put away. They
live together in Swinster, I believe they
may be an item, Sir."

"Ok Kate, good work, let's see what
Wally has for us in the morning."

"Ok sir goodnight."

"Yes goodnight, Kate."

She will make a good DI very soon
Gammon thought after watching her
handle the death of DI Kiernan.

After work John called Saron. She
sounded busy, so he didn't push for a meet
up or anything. Saron was possibly the one
thing in his life he wanted, and could not
have because of his stupidity. Will he ever
get the opportunity to get it right he
thought? He decided to go and see Wez at
the Spinning Jenny. He hadn't been in for
a bit with work and everything. John
walked into the bar area and Tracey
Rodgers was working.

"Hey John, how are you?"

THE MEANING STONES

This is going to be awkward he thought, knowing about India.

"I'm good, Tracey. How things in your life?"

"Oh, a bit same old to be honest. Bit of a turn up Steve moving in though."

"Has he told you what went wrong with Imogen?"

"He just said he made a mistake."

"It was too soon after Jo."

"Well we all knew that John, didn't we? Plus I don't think Imogen was his type, she is a bit of a gold digger. I just hope she doesn't take him for half of what Jo left him or I will be bloody mad."

"What are you having, Pedigree?"

"Yes please, and take one for yourself."

"I'll have a wine, if that's ok?"

"You can whine and moan at me all you want. Most people do at me, Tracey."

"Ha ha, funny guy Gammon."

"Quiet tonight."

"We will be busy in a bit. Lindsay has some friends staying. They have gone for a Chinese then are coming back here.

"She is a lovely girl, don't you think?"

"Yes, they are a nice couple, it's just getting used to Kev and Doreen not being here. I mean they were here when I was growing up, Tracey."

THE MEANING STONES

"So how's the love life, Tracey?"

"Non-existent with this killer on the loose. It's scary. I am sure it will affect tourism in the Peak District at Christmas."

"Well that only gives me seven weeks to find who is doing it, I guess."

"Whoever is doing this has only killed the one guy so far, correct?"

"Don't like the so far Tracey, it implies there is more to come!"

John couldn't truthfully answer her question. He wasn't sure if DI Kiernan was a victim also.

CHAPTER TWO

Unsure of how it happened but he woke next morning to the sound of somebody cooking breakfast.

"How do you like your eggs, John?"

It was Tracey Rodgers.

"Sunny side up, please Tracey."

John put on his dressing gown Tracey had his shirt on and nothing else.

"Nice night, eh."

"Yeah, but how did we end up here?"

"Doreen brought us, and I said I was stopping to put you to bed. Kev and Doreen came in and because Lindsay had

THE MEANING STONES

her friends over you, Kev and Wez opened
a bottle of brandy. Kev said he wanted to
introduce Wez to the delights of a pub
landlord. So we shared a bottle?"

"That wouldn't normally do this to me."

"No, you shared two bottles. Turns out
Wez is a bit of a beer monster. You two
picked on the wrong one last night," and
she laughed as she put John's breakfast in
front of him.

"I will have to get a taxi to pick up my
car."

"Don't worry, Steve is picking me up,
so we can both get our cars."

Great John thought, now Lineman would be giving him stick about Tracey staying. Trouble with Steve he didn't know when to stop and the last thing John wanted was Saron finding out. He knew he had to be squeaky clean if he was to have any chance with her.

True to form Steve texted John after he had picked his car up and left for Bixton.

'You bad man with my sister-in-law hey'.

John didn't text back, or it would be relentless throughout the day.

John arrived at Bixton and told Magic to get the team together in the incident room

THE MEANING STONES

for 9.30am and he headed for his office. It was one of those typical Peak District winter days, a heavy frost in the morning which made Losehill look like something from an Alpine ski holiday brochure.

Gammon was thinking what was the significance of the dice in the eye sockets? Why take of just one eye and was the body being propped against the stone sign significant. He thought not, but maybe it was worth checking out, so he decided to revisit the scene.

Firstly he had the meeting. When Gammon got there the team were assembled.

"Sir?"

"Yes, DI Milton."

"I don't want to sound harsh but when are we getting some help? We are left with me, DI Smarty, DI Lee and DS Yap and Bass."

"Understand Carl, it may take a couple of weeks, but I will sort it."

"Ok Wally, what did you find at the flat of Mr Smidge?"

"Well first thing my people found was a hundred thousand pounds in used twenty pound notes."

There was a gasp in the meeting room.

THE MEANING STONES

"We also found out that Anthony Smidge wasn't Anthony Smidge. He was born Leslie Brough from Hackney London."

"How can that be, Wally? You checked his dental records?"

"The dental records we check are for the last five years, and he visited a dentist in Ackbourne eighteen months ago."

"So how do you know he isn't who he said he was?"

"This," and Wally produced a passport.

"So we are saying this guy moved here and assumed an alias?"

"Certainly looks that way."

Detective John Gammon Series Three
Book Five

"Ok DS Bass, let's find out what you can on Leslie Brough please, and as soon as possible."

"Carl, you help with bank accounts, convictions, anything. We need something on this guy. I mean, why would a guy with a hundred thousand pounds in used notes be working at a cement factory?"

"Anything else, Wally?"

There were pictures of a woman in three separate frames, clearly the same woman. On one of them she was reading a newspaper which dates the picture to eleven month ago."

"Ok DI Lee, find this woman."

THE MEANING STONES

"Anything else?"

"Yes, we found DNA on a breadknife."

"Have we identified the DNA?"

"Not yet, but we are working on it."

"So do we have a future serial killer, a contract killer, or just a maniac, do we think?"

"I'm going with the contract killer."

"Ok Dave. Carl?"

"I'm the same, contract killer. The dice are significant."

Gammon went round the room and it pretty much pointed towards a contract killer.

Detective John Gammon Series Three
Book Five

"Ok thanks everybody, let me know what you find on Leslie Brough."

Gammon grabbed his coat and told Magic he was going out, but should be contactable on his mobile. He drove to Magpie Mine. The setting was stunning with the heavy frost. There were one or two walkers scattered about so Gammon headed straight to the memorial stone that Smidge, as he knew him, was propped up against.

There were three names from the village of Shealdon of men who went to the First World War, but didn't return. Harry Salt, killed at the Battle of Verdun, February 22

THE MEANING STONES

1916, Thomas Myers, killed at the Battle of the Somme, August 3 1916. Then another name which hadn't weathered well, but Gammon though it said Walter Plantager, killed at the Battle of Amiens August 1 1918. Gammon made note of all three names in case they had any significance. He decided to have lunch at the Broken Egg and see if any old locals knew the story of the men.

Gammon walked in and to his surprise Steve was sitting with India Green eating lunch. This could be embarrassing he thought.

"Hey John, you know India."

India looked stunning and she smiled with those brilliant white teeth.

"We came here, out of the way, with things as they are at the moment mate."

"Look, don't think I'm being funny, I will let you get your lunch. I'm only grabbing a sandwich and need to talk to some locals."

John thought both Steve and India were relieved that he wasn't going to sit with them.

John perched himself at the bar where two old lads were sat talking.

"Could I have a pint of Steers please and I will take one of those ham cobs please?"

THE MEANING STONES

"That will be four pounds forty seven please, Sir."

John paid the young girl.

The two guys said hello.

"Oh hi, I wondered do you both live in the village?"

"Yes, we do. Been friends ever since we started school together on the same day and that was eighty five years ago."

"Oh wow, so you are both ninety then?"

"Yes both born on the same date as well November 13."

"Blimey, I'm John."

"We know who you are you are, that famous detective, aren't you?"

"Not sure about famous, Mr?"

"I'm Chris Tuttle and my mate is Arthur Denby. You will have to excuse Arthur, he is a bit deaf, Mr Gammon."

"Oh, that's ok Chris, call me John. You know about the murder up at Magpie Mine?"

"Yes, rum do that. I think everybody is thinking this will affect visitors come the Christmas period. Laura and Gary, the landlord and landlady at the Broken Egg, said they have had three cancellations for rooms in the last week."

"The three names on the memorial stone, did you know much about them?

THE MEANING STONES

Have they any living relatives in the village?"

"Thomas Myers and Walter Plantager were only seventeen and their families left maybe fifty year ago. Harry Salt on the other hand was twenty four when he died. He was married with one son, also called Harry. He lived in Magpie House about five doors down from the pub. He was only a baby when his dad died, and he died twenty years back. He also had a son called Harry. It was some kind of tradition to name the boy after Harry who died in the First World War, like a mark of respect, John. His son is about forty eight and now lives in that house, well that's when he isn't down London. He works for the Gaming Commission, or something like that."

All the time they were talking Arthur was nodding in agreement with Chris Tuttle.

"Interesting lads, let me buy you both a drink, and I best get back to work."

The two old lads thanked Gammon and he left returning to the station.

Gammon spoke with DI Milton and told him about Harry Salt of the London Gaming Commission, and the connection

THE MEANING STONES

with the stone where Leslie Brough was found.

"Ok Sir, I'll get on it right away. Wally found the DNA to be that of a Marilyn Kaiser. I ran the name through the data base, and she was convicted twenty years ago for supplying prostitutes in London. She was recently, and I am sure this is only by chance, but she was in the Micklock Mercury. They had done an article on a new coffee shop in Swinster called Dolly Buns and Coffee. I was reading about it at lunchtime and recognised the picture in the frame from the flat."

Milton showed Gammon the article.

"Blimey Carl, it must be our lucky day.
Get digging on Harry Salt while I talk with
Kaiser."

Gammon set off for Swinster, the drive
was always special he thought. The Peak
District didn't have the bright lights of
London, but it had beauty and solitude. He
arrived in Swinster and decided to park at
the Spinning Jenny and walk down East
Bank, or Jiggers Hill as the locals called it,
although nobody seemed to know why
anymore. At the bottom he found The
Dolly Bun Café. It was housed in what
was some sixty years ago the Angel pub. It

THE MEANING STONES

wasn't particularly big although pleasantly fitted out. Marilyn Kaiser came over. Gammon recognised her instantly.

"Marilyn Kaiser, DCI Gammon," and he flashed his warrant card.

"How can I help you?"

Kaiser was mid-forties but had kept her looks and maintained a good figure.

"Can we talk privately?"

"Sure."

"Wendy, watch the café I need to speak with Mr Gammon."

She showed him into her back office. On the walls were pictures of celebrities with her hung round their necks.

Interesting he thought.

"Did you know an Anthony Smidge?"

"Why are you asking me this question?"

"Please just answer the question, Miss Kaiser."

"Yes, I know Tony."

"How long have you known him for?"

Kaiser hesitated.

"About eight years."

"Did you know him when he lived in London?"

"I'm not sure where this is leading. I think it would be best if I had a solicitor present."

THE MEANING STONES

"Before you make that decision Miss Kaiser, a couple of days ago Anthony Smidge was found murdered."

Kaiser looked generally shocked.

"On investigation it was discovered that he wasn't Anthony Smidge, but Leslie Brough."

"With further investigation we also found out you had been convicted for keeping an illegal house for sexual pleasures. So Miss Kaiser, if you wish I can take you to the station now, and you can have your solicitor, or you can help right now in trying to find Mr Brough's killer. What's it to be?"

Kaiser didn't hesitate.

"About eight years ago I lived with
Leslie in Camden London. We met at a
party thrown by Lady Isabella Frobisher.
Leslie was a known underworld associate.
He would often come to my place for what
we called comfort time. At the party we
danced and laughed. He was a very good
looking man in those days and I fell in
love with him. The problem was, Leslie
wasn't in love with me. We lived together
for about eighteen months. He never asked
about my business and I never asked about
his."

THE MEANING STONES

"One Sunday afternoon he came home. I had been working a lot of the night, so I was still in bed. He woke me and said we had to leave. The urgency in his voice scared me. I asked why, and he said he couldn't tell me, but we had to go now. I started to pack but he stopped me. He said we leave now leave everything other than money and passports. He grabbed my arm and said, if we don't leave now I am a dead man and because of your association you will be too."

"Leslie had a Porsche 911and we drove as far as Birmingham. He pulled into a garage and swapped it for Ford Sierra.

Detective John Gammon Series Three
Book Five

From memory I think the guy gave him the car and three hundred pounds. The sales guy must have thought all his birthdays had come at once."

"He hardly spoke on the journey and he certainly wasn't in the mood for questions for sure. We arrived in a place called Swinster and called at The Spinning Jenny. We said we were up on holiday and could they recommend anywhere. The landlord said he was fully booked but we could try Tiffany Watson in the village. Then he kindly rang the lady and we stayed for two weeks before renting something permanent."

THE MEANING STONES

"I remember it was a hot summer's day, we had been in Derbyshire about three months, and he took a call from somebody. Leslie was gone ten minutes, so I went in to get a cold beer. The spare bedroom door was ajar, so I pushed it open. To my utter surprise he had bundles of money, and I mean bundles of money. I asked him what it was, but he stormed into a rage calling me names like whore and skank. In fact anything that could hurt me, I guess. I started crying and said I was leaving him. I had a little cleaning job working with my friend Wendy. We became great friends so I rang her and said we had split. I never told her why. I knew that money had to be hot."

"I never saw Leslie, or Tony as was then, until about six month ago. He came to see me. By then I had rented a flat off a cousin of Wendy's who was working in Italy for five years. He just knocked on my door. At first I didn't recognise the dishevelled man in orange overalls covered in cement dust. I asked him in, but even then I felt anger towards him. I had given my life up to be with him and now I was cleaning to get by, unsure where my next fiver would come from."

THE MEANING STONES

"He sat at the kitchen table and broke down. He then told me about what he had done. He said he had been an enforcer for Johnny Guitar Lomax, so called because he was always trying to play the guitar, with little success I might add, but nobody would dare to say that to him."

"Leslie told me that he had murdered twelve or thirteen people in the years he had been Johnnie's enforcer. He had tortured numerous other men and women which he said he was ashamed of. He said after he met me he tried to break away, but Johnny had told him I was unfaithful to him, which just wasn't true. He said that's why he acted like he didn't love me."

"He said Johnny told him the only way he would be allowed to leave was in a box going the crematorium. He said we had to leave that afternoon was because he had been an enforcer on a drug deal at Newhaven. Drugs were coming in and it was his job to ensure that the seven hundred and fifty thousand pounds that Johnny was handing over for the drugs was all done correctly."

"I don't suppose it matters now but Leslie said he shot the three boat dealers and one of the other minders that Johnny

THE MEANING STONES

had sent with him. He said he couldn't shoot little Gary Birch because he liked Gary. So he gave him the drugs, wished him well, then tied him up and put him on the boat to give him time to get back to me, and get away. He knew, excuse the pun, that he had now burned his bridges. He said he never touched the money while Johnny Guitar was alive. He then said a few months ago that he had bought a small café in Swinster under my name and paid for it. He was leaving, and I would never see him again. He wouldn't tell me where, he said that was safer for me. He said it would be suspicious if he did not see out his shift the next night. Then he would just disappear because he saw on the news that Lomax was dead."

"He told me he had one chance to get away with the seven hundred and fifty thousand he had never touched until he bought the café for me."

At this point Marilyn Kaiser's hard exterior evaporated and she cried. Gammon gave her a white handkerchief.

"I'm glad you have told me this here, and not at the station Marilyn. I may need to question you some more, but at the station, as far as I am concerned, I know nothing of the café and how it was bought.

THE MEANING STONES

But I do want to find who killed Leslie Brough. I will be in touch," and he gave her a card to contact him if she needed.

Just as he was leaving, he asked Kaiser why did they end up here in The Peak District? She said Leslie just liked it.

Gammon was quite pleased with his day's work and was keen to get his teeth into all the information he had.

It was only 4.30pm but John had enough for the day. There was one place he needed to go, and that was the Spinning Jenny with the intention of seeing if Lindsay would do him a take-away as Doreen always had in the past. He had just got on the car-park when his phone rang.

It was DI Smarty.

"Hi Dave, I have just called it a night. In fact just pulled on the car park at the Spinning Jenny, if you fancy a quick one?"

"Thanks for the offer mate, but me and the wife are taking French lessons and it's the first class tonight."

"Ok mate, no problem."

"All it was John, we had DCI Bembridge from Scotland Yard. He said Mr and Mrs Kiernan wish to have Danny buried at Little Dove which is in Staffordshire where they live. They said the funeral was arranged for 2.30pm this Thursday. DCI Bembridge said he would like three officers that Danny served with in Scotland Yard and three from Bixton police to carry the coffin. He also asked if you would do a eulogy as he was away on holiday after today. I said I thought that would be ok John, hope you don't mind?"

"Not at all mate. I will speak in the morning."

John walked into the bar. Wez and Tracey Rodgers were behind the bar. Phil Sterndale was sitting with his back against the post. Carol Lestar and her mum Freda were sitting by the fire, and the rest of the room was full of holiday makers.

"Hey John, get this man a pint of your best Pedigree, please Wez."

"Will do, Phil."

"Thanks Phil, how are you mate?"

"Oh, been better."

"What, have you been poorly?"

"No, just me and Sheba haven't been getting along."

"Why's that?"

"My fault, I had been seeing somebody on the side."

"Really, who?"

"Well she is an old school flame."

THE MEANING STONES

"Go on then, what's her name? Or do I have to guess?"

"I don't think you will need to guess, she is meeting me here tonight for a meal. Her name is Linda Marston, she is from Bucket near Buxton."

Carol Lestar came to the bar.

"How's my favourite copper? Will you come over and have a chat with Mum? This is the first time she has been out properly since our trip to America."

Carol winked at him like only Carol could, trying to be discreet because John paid for the treatment. Phil smiled. Most people knew about John's generosity by now.

"Excuse me Phil, I best just have a quick word with Freda."

"Go ahead mate, Linda will be here in a minute anyhow."

John wandered over and thought how well Freda looked. She got up and threw her arms round him.

"I haven't had chance to thank you for all you have done for me. Your Mum and Dad would have been proud. Carol get John a drink."

THE MEANING STONES

"You are ok Freda, I had a few too many last night so only popped in for a quick pint and a take away."

"Ok lad, then some other time. I can recommend Lindsay's suet pudding; bloody lovely it was, wasn't it Carol?"

"Yes mam, it was great."

"Thanks, I might try that. Enjoy the rest of your night and its lovely to see you so well again, Freda."

John got back to the bar just has Phil and his new beau Linda were headed for the restaurant. Phil introduced Linda, who seemed quite shy. John ordered one more

Pedigree then asked Tracey if she thought
Lindsay would do him a take away.

"I'll do better than that. I finish at
8.30pm. If you hang on, I'll come with
you and cook something."

Fresh food cooked by the delectable
Tracey was hard to turn down.

The pub was reasonably busy as John
set off to warm the car up. Tracey arrived
clutching a bag of food from the pub.

"Wasn't sure you would want me
cooking all night? I thought we could have
this and then enjoy the night together."

It wasn't what John had planned, but
being the man he was, he wasn't about to

THE MEANING STONES

turn it down. Besides, Miss Rodgers was a very pretty girl with a figure to match.

They got back, and she had brought two lasagnes with a salad. Not quite the suet pudding he had fancied, but hey lasagne brought to you on a plate, with a glass of red, by a beautiful woman. John would have been hard pressed to beat that.

They talked for a long time about Jo, Imogen and Steve. John really wanted to tell her about India, but he felt that was his mate's place.

"Are you taking me to bed policeman hunk?" she enquired.

She freshened up and they were soon in
bed. Being a good boy for Saron was
wearing thin; a man's got to do what a
man's got to do.

They had almost three hours of pure lust
and sex. She said afterward she wanted no
ties and that suited John. She was the
probably the first woman not to try and tie
him down so that felt good.

They finally fell asleep at 3.10am, but
Tracey was up at 7.00am cooking John a
bacon sandwich. He followed the bacon
smell to the kitchen. She was standing
with just one of John's John Rocha shirts
and a pair black stiletto heels. The

inevitable happened in the confines of the kitchen this time.

John took Tracey, with his bacon sandwich to eat on the way, to the Spinning Jenny for her car.

Arriving at Bixton John told Magic to get everyone in the incident room at 9.00am. He grabbed a quick coffee and was obviously feeling quite tired after the night's exploits.

"Ok everyone. First of all, Danny Kiernan's funeral is in Staffordshire. DI Smarty took a call yesterday. Three of his colleagues from Scotland Yard will carry

the coffin, and I would like three
volunteers from Bixton please. The funeral
is Thursday. Anybody wishing to attend,
with it just being over the border from
Derbyshire, please let me know so we can
still ensure we are manned ok here."

DS Bass put her hand up.

"I would like to, Sir."

"Ok Kate."

DI Smarty and DI Lee also volunteered.

"Ok well, anybody that would just like
to go give your names to PC Magic. He
has all the details."

THE MEANING STONES

"Ok with that sad bit of news let's move on. DS Bass, what have we got on Leslie Brough?"

"He was a known criminal in London about ten years ago. He managed to get off an ABH charge as the witness declined to testify. Then about eight years ago he disappeared off the radar. Speaking with Scotland Yard, the word on the street was that he was murdered by Johnny Guitar Lomax for stealing seven hundred and fifty thousand pounds off him."

"Well that doesn't add up Kate, we only found one hundred thousand in his flat."

"Maybe in the eight years he spent it?"

"Carl?"

"A lot of money to spend in eight years, Sir."

"Perhaps he had expensive tastes?"

"Don't forget he was trying to blend into the background here in the Peak District."

"Kate, have you looked into this Johnny Guitar Lomax?"

"As much as I could. He was low profile, but very high in the underworld my source said. I only found one bank account, but typically that was squeaky clean. His other accounts are probably off shore under a different name."

THE MEANING STONES

"Ok well, I want you to find a guy called Gary Birch. He is a known associate of Lomax I am told."

Gammon didn't want to tell everyone the full story. Marilyn Krieger was trying hard to get her life in gear and, if possible, he would leave her out of it.

"I want this Gary Birch tracing, and I need to question him. You sort that please Kate."

"DI Lee, I want you to discreetly find what you can on a Harry Salt. He lives in Shealdon at Magpie House but spends most of his time in London. He works for the Gaming Commission. I want his bank accounts looking into. I want to know who his friends are, especially in London. I need as much as I can on this guy please Peter."

He left the meeting, then remembered his suit needed cleaning for the funeral. Just by a stroke of luck Tracey called.

"Hey, what are you doing tonight? I thought I might cook you a proper evening meal if you wanted?"

"That would be great. Are you working today?"

"No, why?"

"Could you do me a favour? I need my black Armani suit cleaning. I have a

THE MEANING STONES

funeral on Thursday. Is there any chance you could go and get it, and drop it off at the one day cleaners in Ackbourne?"

"That's no problem John. Where is the key?"

"Go round the back, and it's under a wooden planter."

"Ok, no problem. That's good because I could then get your evening meal ready for when you get back."

"Look Tracey, I feel bad. Let me treat you to a meal. They do nice meals now at Up the steps Maggie's."

"Ooh, now that would be nice. So shall I wait at yours?"

"Yes, that would be good. Should be back about 6.15pm, if all goes to plan."

John was true to his word and arrived back spot on time. Tracey had a black, tight dress cut above the knee which accentuated her curves. John quickly showered, and they were on their way by 6.45pm. It wasn't too busy with only a few tables with reserved signs on them. They sat down, and John ordered a bottle of red.

"What do you fancy?"

"Not sure John, it all looks good."

"Would you like a starter?"

"No, I'm fine. I prefer a dessert to be honest."

THE MEANING STONES

The young girl came over and took their order. Tracey made John laugh, she was very relaxed. They finished the first bottle just as Tracey's lamb shank and John's shepherd's pie arrived.

As the waitress turned to leave their table as John heard a giggle. He would know that anywhere he thought.

"John, who's that with Saron?"

John looked across. Saron looked stunning in white trousers, brown boots, a light blue tight fitting top and her blonde hair cascading over her shoulders.

"I don't know, Tracey."

"Did you know she would be here?"

"No, of course not."

"Well, don't take this the wrong way, she looks well over you. Look at her holding onto him and smiling, John."

John could feel the envy pulsing through his veins. It was hard not to take his eyes off of her. She looked so happy and he wasn't sure if she had even seen him, so the show wasn't for him.

As the desserts arrived Saron and the mystery guy were leaving, and she spotted John, He noticed she let go of the guy's hand. He wasn't sure if that was a sign she still had feelings, or just a look at me, I don't care. She smiled at John and said hello to Tracey.

It somewhat ruined the night and Tracey Rodgers could feel it. They arrived John's place.

"Look John, I'm not staying tonight. I can see the Saron thing upset you and I understand you aren't over her, and I get that. Just give me a call if anytime you fancy a night out. Like I said, no strings."

She drove away, and John felt terrible. She was a strong woman and possibly the first one he had ever taken out that didn't want to form a relationship.

CHAPTER THREE

The following day John called DI Lee and DS Bass to his office.

"What have we got on Birch and Salt?"

"Well, first Gary Birch became the enforcer for Lomax after Leslie Brough did a runner. So there is motive with Birch, his dislike for Brough, and maybe the hit was ordered by Lomax which would have been carried out by Birch with him being his enforcer. He lives at number thirty three, Treacle Crescent in Greenwich, London, Sir. I have spoken with Scotland Yard and they want to speak with you."

"Ok, do you have a name?"

"Yes Sir, DI Coglan."

"Yes, I know Billy Coglan... What have you got, DI Lee, on Harry Salt?"

"Well he doesn't appear to have too many associates down in London, but he does make a payment to a Marina Dalia of around one hundred and thirty five pounds a week."

"Do we know who Maria Dalia is, DI Lee?"

"I checked the Police database with it being an unusual name and guess what?

She is an escort. She was involved in a court case about three years ago and lost it in the witness box when the defence lawyer questioned her about, as he put it, being on the game. She blurted out that it was men like the judge that used escorts, so he was not to be so patronising. The judge soon got her off the witness stand."

"That's great DI Lee, so Harry Salt is using escorts? He could be compromised in his job, this gets better by the minute. Right I suggest we get Harry Salt in for questioning. I'll leave that with you Peter just let me know when."

THE MEANING STONES

"Kate, I'll phone DI Coglan now and you may as well be party to the conversation."

Gammon rang Coglan.

"Billy? John Gammon."

"Hey John, how are you? How's life in the back of beyond? I hear on the grapevine you made DCI."

"Only acting DCI, mate."

"Well done mate, you were always going to get to the top."

"Kind of you to say mate."

"When DS Bass called I thought it must have been at your request."

Detective John Gammon Series Three
Book Five

"Yes mate, I need as much on Gary Birch as you can give me. If possible, and if you don't mind, I could send DS Bass and DI Milton down to interview him."

"No problem to me John, but what's your thought pattern on Little Gary Birch? I have been wanting to nail him for many years."

"Well, a guy was murdered, and his eyes gouged out and replaced with two dice. One eye was left, and one was taken we assume by the perpetrator."

"Wow, some nasty shit then mate, and you think Birch could have been involved?"

THE MEANING STONES

"Yes, I do mate."

"Ok, well let me do some digging. When did this happen?"

"Four nights ago."

"Ok, let's see if he was in London on that date mate first."

"Brilliant Billy, thanks for your help."

"It will cost you. Are you attending young Danny Kiernan's funeral?"

"I'm going and three of my officers are carrying the coffin."

"Ok, well I may have something by then, so we can have a chat after the funeral."

"Thanks Billy, see you Thursday."

It was getting to late afternoon when a man came into the station. Magic called up to Gammon.

"You might want to talk with this gentleman at the front desk. His name is Harbey Clayton. He said his friend Robert Bloom has been missing from their home for two days."

"I'm on my way down. Put him in interview room one please, Magic."

Gammon collared Smarty.

"You best come and listen to this, Dave."

Clayton would have been in his mid-sixties John thought. He was dressed in corduroys and a light blue Harrington jacket, very Marks and Spencer's John thought.

"How can I help you, Mr Clayton? I'm DCI Gammon and this is DI Smarty."

"It's my partner, Mr Gammon, he went missing two days ago."

"Could he have gone to see friends? Had you been arguing?"

"No, me and Robert never argued. We were, sorry, are happy."

Gammon noticed the unintentional slip into the past tense that made him feel uncomfortable. Clayton was continually

biting his nails and his fingers were very
badly stained from nicotine.

"Do you have a current picture of Mr
Bloom please, Mr Clayton?"

Clayton felt in his jacket and produced a
photograph of him and Bloom.

"This was taken a few month ago we
went on a Mediterranean cruise."

"Ok well, PC Magic has your address.
We will circulate this and try and find
your partner."

"You don't understand. He took a phone
call from somebody before he
disappeared."

"Did he say who it was?"

THE MEANING STONES

"All he said to me was, the past should stay in the past, but he was concerned."

"What do you think he may have meant?"

"I might as well tell you. We ran Casinos back in the day and knew a lot of the underworld. We both went to prison for fiddling the tax man. When we came out, we decided to get away from that life, so we settled up here where nobody knew us."

"Were you beholden to any of the underworld?"

Clayton hesitated for a minute.

"Listen, if I tell you something it's strictly between us."

"Robert was quite the boy, but bi-sexual. He got one of the big hitter's daughters pregnant."

"What was her name?"

"Amelia Lomax, Johnny Guitar's daughter. He put a contract out on Robert. When he was inside they nearly succeeded, he was in hospital for almost a year. That was the reason we came to live here. When we heard Lomax had passed away we were both relieved, but then Robert got that call. I'm sure it has a bearing Mr Gammon."

THE MEANING STONES

"Ok, leave it with us please, Mr Clayton."

They showed Clayton out.

"This is falling into place, Dave. All roads keep leading back to Lomax and his enforcer Little Gary Birch. Hopefully DI Coglan will have something for me. Who was the other guy at Scotland Yard?"

"Oh, Bembridge."

"I don't know him, he must be new, Dave."

Gammon was about to go back to his office when Magic stopped him.

"There has been another incident, Sir."

"Where Magic?"

"Just outside Truffles Farm, near Shealdon."

"Get me a postcode and send Wally and the team."

"Come on Dave, grab your coat. I have a feeling this could be Bob Bloom."

The team set off and found two women by the body, both very upset.

"DCI Gammon," he flashed his warrant card.

"Which one of you ladies called us?"

"That was me, Sonia was too upset."

"You are?"

THE MEANING STONES

"Verity Sigma, and this is my friend Sonia Cutts. We are on holiday, we live in Boston, Lincolnshire."

Wally started setting up his white tent. The body was propped up against a stone.

"We often walk up here, Mr Gammon, it's so beautiful."

"Yes, it is a lovely spot. Have you touched the body?"

"I was going to, but Sonia stopped me."

"Good, so the crime scene hasn't been compromised. Look ladies I am very sorry for your experience. DI Smarty will take your details so if we need to contact you we can."

Gammon left Smarty take the details and he put his head inside the tent. It was guaranteed that Wally would usher him out for fear of him contaminating the crime scene.

"What did the stone say that he was propped up against, Wally?"

'Take a while to sit and view

The wonders of nature given but not due

Take your time and sit a while

For life will leave you without a smile

Your time will come but oh so quick

And leave a memory made of stick

The stick will break and so will you

THE MEANING STONES

So enjoy now my friend for life is not just for you'

"There was one eye left on the stone and both his eyes have been replaced by dice, John. Other than that you will have to wait until the morning. And before you say it, yes I will be ready at 9.00am in the incident room."

"Thanks Wally."

"Dave, do you fancy a quick drink in the Broken Egg?"

"Will have to just be one mate, got another French lesson tonight."

They arrived at the Broken Egg and for 5.15pm it was quite busy.

"Hey up love," said the bubbly landlady. "Aren't you those coppers from Bixton?"

"Yes we are."

"Rum do about Truffles Field. Hey who was he?"

Bloody hell Gammon thought, news travels fast in these little villages.

"We are investigating it, but can I ask how you knew so quickly?"

"He was found in Joe Gilbraith's field. Him sat over there. His lad runs the farm now so old Joe is in here from 4.30pm until closing. Right, what can I get you?"

"What do you fancy Dave?"

"That looks good, Doodlebug."

THE MEANING STONES

"Yes, selling well my friend."

"Ok, let's have two of them."

John and Dave got their pints and sat down at the same table as Joe Gilbraith. Old Joe had a mac on, tied round the waist with orange baler twine and it had dried cow muck on it. On his head he had an orange woolly hat with Bensons feedstock emblazoned across the front of it.

"Afternoon, Joe isn't it?"

"Aye and tha a copper, can smell you buggar's a mile off."

That's rich coming from a person smelling of cow muck John thought but didn't say.

"Yes, I believe the body of the gentleman was found in your field."

"Yes, it was in Stone Field. My grandad had that stone put there in 1888."

"What was the significance of the stone?"

"They ward off evil, if that what tha asking with your fancy words. My family have farmed this land for eight generations tha knows. Problem now is the bloody walkers can walk anywhere, since they had that major walk thing on Kinder Scout in protest about private land."

It was clear old Joe didn't have much to say so they finished their drinks, said

THE MEANING STONES

goodnight and Smarty went off to his French class.

John decided to go the Tow'd Man. It was bugging him who the guy Saron was with the other night.

The car park was empty, not unusual for this time of year and the run up to Christmas. John parked and walked the short distance across the car-park down the stone steps into the bar area. Donna was behind the bar and Saron was sitting by the fire with that guy again. She looked surprised to see John, but did put her hand up and acknowledge him whilst the guy scowled.

"Hey John, nice to see you. What can I get you?"

"I'll have a pint of Bass please, Donna. Who's the guy?"

"Oh, that's Sheridan Branch, you know Branch Soft Drinks in Ackbourne. Saron met him when we were invited to a factory tour. We buy all our soft drink from them. He is flippin' loaded."

"Is that his Ferrari outside?"

"Possibly, he has more cars than I do underwear, John. Why the interest? I thought you and Saron were done with?"

"Oh yeah, just wondered."

THE MEANING STONES

"I know you better John Gammon, I detect a bit of jealousy."

"No, nothing like that, Donna."

"Well you did treat her rough John, and she has to move on at some point. So anyway, we are having Christmas party. You know, disco with Tony Maloney spinning the hits, and a Christmas buffet. It's in aid of Swinster Village Hall. Fifteen pound a ticket this Saturday. I know its early, but we will be rammed when the lead up to Christmas comes."

"Give me two, Donna."

"Ooh, got a new lady to bring, have we?"

John just tapped his nose and smiled. He had every intention of bringing somebody he thought. There was no way he would let Saron upstage him. He drank his drink and called at the chip shop in Hittington for fish and chips for his tea.

John sat looking out towards his back garden beginning to realise that he had probably lost Saron now, and he had to get on with his life. The party night might be a good place to start.

The following morning the team assembled in the incident room.

THE MEANING STONES

"Ok everybody, listen up. It's Danny's funeral today so all you that have been allocated the time I suggest we leave around 12.15pm. Ok now, Wally if you could come up and tell us what you found yesterday."

Wally came to the front.

"He is a white male approximately sixty seven years old. His eyes were removed, and two dice were placed there. On the last victim the dice were set at two sixes these dice were set at two fives. There was one eye left, and the killer we assume, like the last victim took the other one. The victim was Robert Bloom. There is no

DNA on the victim. He still had a wallet with money and credit cards, so this wasn't a robbery gone wrong."

"Ok thank you, Wally."

"Right, what do we have?" and he wrote Bob Bloom below the first victim, Leslie Brough.

"We have two victims, both had been in the Casino gambling industry, both fled London to the Peak District. Why?"

"Yes, DI Smarty?"

"Clearly they both had a contract on them, but the killer is making it look like we have a serial killer."

"Yes, DS Bass?"

THE MEANING STONES

"The dice Sir, does this mean there will be six murders, do we think?"

"Good point Kate, I think your assumption could be correct."

"Yes, DI Lee?"

"What with taking one eye and leaving one. I think this is possibly to trick us into thinking we have a serial killer lose in the Peak District where what we have is a contract killer."

"Let's look at what we have, which is very little. Little Gary Birch is our main suspect. I am hoping to have something on him this afternoon, and old colleague from the yard is going to give me some information, I hope. Everything points back to Johnny Guitar Lomax and Birch. We have one more suspect which I think we should pull in tomorrow. That's Harry Salt, he lives sometimes in Shealdon and will know the area. He is involved with escorts and works at the Gaming Commission. Could he be covering his tracks?"

"Ok everybody, those attending our colleague's funeral let's meet in reception at 12.15pm please."

"Oh, before you go Wally, did the victim have a mobile phone on him?"

"Didn't find one?"

THE MEANING STONES

"Damn, that would have the mystery caller's voice on it."

"DS Yap, get the phone records for Clayton's phone and let's see if we can identify a number around the time Clayton took the call."

12.15pm arrived and Bass, Smarty and Lee along with Gammon left for the funeral at Little Dove in Staffordshire. DS Bass chose to drive. She dropped John at the church to meet with the funeral directors. John walked in church which was quite full. He had scribbled down a eulogy for Danny. He thought to himself that he was getting good at these things the

amount of funerals he attended. The coffin
was brought into 'The Sound of Silence'
by Simon and Garfunkel. The service was
good, well good as funeral services can be.
It was time for John to do his Eulogy.

"Ladies and gentleman and Danny's
family, I was asked to speak on behalf of
Scotland Yard and Bixton police.
Although I didn't know Danny that well,
he was an excellent officer and we are
proud to have served with him. Danny had
an enormous amount of energy for the job
and was destined for the top, of that I am
sure. I suppose generally people stand here
and say something that reminds us of the

person whose life they are celebrating. I really don't have many funny stories that I guess you could all relate to other than this one."

"Danny had been at Bixton for two days when he knocked on my door. Come in I stated. In strode Danny all efficient looking. Good Morning Sir says Danny. Yes Good Morning DI Kiernan how can I help you? I was told by DI Smarty and DI Lee to check out a suspect and that he would be attending the Hook a Duck Carnival event on Low Edge waters near Puddle Dale. They said the man would be wearing a cap. I must admit I had all on

not laughing. Go on Danny I said. Well I
arrived in good time and waited. People
started arriving and they were all kids, but
they all had flat caps on. I was confused. I
have come back to the station, but PC
Magic said they are out on another case. I
am concerned we may lose a key witness,
so I thought I better tell you. Well thank
you for that and welcome to the Peak
District which you will find is full of
characters, customs and fun. I'm afraid
you were set up Danny. That's when I saw
the serious side of Danny. He wasn't
amused although me being his chief, he
played it down."

THE MEANING STONES

"So in my mind we have lost a good copper, a nice person and a model professional."

John left the pulpit.

Back at the Red Lion, the village inn chosen for the wake, John briefly spoke with Danny's mum. DI Bainbridge wanted to talk, so he left to find DI Billy Coglan. Coglan had always liked a tipple and today was going to be no different.

"Hey John, good to see you mate."

John pulled Billy aside.

"What have you got for me?"

"Gary Birch wasn't in London on the dates you gave me. Word on the streets is he was on a hit."

"Really? So where is he now? Can you bring him in for questioning, Billy?

"It won't be easy, I mean what do I bring him in on? I can't go on hearsay, can I?"

"Billy, get him on anything, a bloody traffic offence, and I will get DS Bass and DI Smarty down to question him. If they feel we have grounds to bring him to Derbyshire they will let you know."

"Ok, get your officers down to Scotland Yard tomorrow for 11.00am, John."

THE MEANING STONES

"Billy, you are a star mate, thank you."

Gammon wandered over to Bass and Smarty.

"When you get back get an overnight bag. I want you in Scotland Yard to question Gary Birch. He wasn't in London on the dates of the murders and word is he was doing a hit. Ensure you are there for 11.00am."

"Wow Sir, you have some pull still down in London."

"Just old friends Kate, doing me a favour."

"I'm impressed, Sir."

"Look, you and Smarty get back and get down to London. Then in the morning go to Scotland Yard and ask for DI Coglan. He will have the interview set up with Birch. If you feel there is more to come ask for a transfer of Birch to Bixton for further questioning."

"Ok Sir, and thank you for having faith in me."

"Not a problem Kate, just don't let me down."

Gammon thought it fair he should get back to Swinster to go and see Harbey Clayton, and give him the news about Robert Bloom his long-time partner.

THE MEANING STONES

Gammon arrived back in Swinster. It was a cold night with a full moon. Swinster was a village that had stood the test of time. The beautiful old Market House dating back to the sixteenth century stood proudly in the centre of the village. The little shop typified and English shop with its ornate Dickensian windows decorated for the coming Christmas time. The paths were all cobbled and driving past the old Market House Gammon had to do a sharp left up a winding lane. The houses all seemed small, and they appeared to cling to either side of the steep hill, as if their very being depended on it.

Clayton's house was an old dairy that had been converted in the sixties. Gammon just managed to park his car, as the hill didn't lend itself to motor powered vehicles.

He knocked only the old oak door which Clayton answered almost immediately.

"Mr Gammon, do come in. I was just about to pour a glass of sherry; would you care to join me?"

"I'm fine Mr Clayton, thank you. I'm afraid I have some bad news."

"It's Robert, isn't it? They have caught up with him, haven't they?"

THE MEANING STONES

"Whoever they are, yes. I'm afraid Mr Bloom was found today at a place called Truffles Field. We are treating it as murder."

Surprisingly Clayton was quiet calm.

"I'm sorry to have to ask you this, and I know you told me Mr Bloom was bisexual and he had a child by Mr Lomax's daughter, were you aware of any other enemies?"

"Ooh, Robert had loads. When Bobby was in town all the old queens blew a fuse. Their partners hated him, he was so good looking," Clayton said sipping his sherry with his little finger sticking out.

"I will have to ask you to officially identify the body. Would you need us to pick you up?"

"No, I will be fine, but thank you."

"Do you need any grief counselling?"

"Only if he is twenty five with a six pack and likes old queens."

Gammon really didn't know what to say, so he simply said goodnight to Clayton.

Seeing that The Spinning Jenny was at the top of the hill leading out of Swinster John felt compelled to call for a swift drink. As was the norm lately the pub was busy. Phil and his new girlfriend Linda

THE MEANING STONES

were sitting at the bar with Bob and Cheryl, Rita and Tony, Tracey Rodgers, Carol Lestar, Jack and Shelley, and Kev and Doreen.

"Blimey, what are you lot all doing here?"

"Kev's birthday. I rang the station and they said you were at a funeral, so I left a message with the front desk to say we were meeting here at 6.00pm."

"Never got it Doreen, sorry."

"Never mind, you are here now."

"So what do you think of the Christmas decorations, John?"

"Very good Wez, but it's not quite December yet."

"Will be Saturday mate," and Wez laughed as he went pouring drinks for the gathering.

"Which reminds me, are you going to Saron's pre-Christmas party Saturday?"

John knew Carol Lestar was prying.

"Yes, got two tickets, taking Miss Rodgers, aren't I, Tracey?"

Tracey almost choked on her drink but knew what John was doing.

"Yes, looking forward to it, John."

Carol's nose had been put out of joint. Her news about Saron and her new bloke wouldn't have same impact, but she wasn't going to let that deter her.

"Saron's got a new bloke, they reckon he is a millionaire."

John knew what the crack was.

"Yes, she is seeing Sheridan Branch, his father owns the soft drinks place in Ackbourne. He seems like a nice guy."

Carol was totally knocked off her perch with John's reply.

Tracey wandered over to John determined to make the most of his comments.

"So, are you having a mini bus Saturday night?"

"Yes, all organised John. I assumed you were coming. We leave the Spinning Jenny at 7.30pm, but thought we could all meet about 6.30pm for a drink."

"Sounds like a plan, Tracey."

John stood talking to Kev.

"So you lost the lovely Saron to a millionaire, eh mate?"

"Not lost anything yet Kev. It's early days mate, don't underestimate me."

"I would certainly never do that, but if you pull this one round, I would be incredibly impressed."

"Let's have a bottle of Brandy on this."

"Go on then, what's the bet?"

THE MEANING STONES

"I bet you I am back with Saron by New Year's Eve."

"I'll take that bet my friend."

John had missed Kev since he came out of the pub. They were close and John could tell him anything, and being older he seemed to have the wisdom to point him in the right direction.

Jackie and Cheryl had made Kev a big birthday cake and Doreen was determined he would cut it and give a speech.

"All Kev's friends, he is now going to cut the cake and then my lovely husband will make a speech."

Everybody clapped. Kev left John's side with his face bright red.

He cut the cake.

"I would like to thank Doreen for a lovely evening. Cheryl and Jackie for this awesome cake, then of course all of you for being here tonight to celebrate this old fart's birthday. Thank you"

"Music please maestro," Doreen shouted, and the disco kicked up with 'Dancing Queen' by Abba. Tracey grabbed John to dance.

"What was that all about?"

"Oh, you know how Carol is. She was just digging for info on me and Saron."

THE MEANING STONES

"Is there any info, John."

"No, absolutely not, she has moved on and I have."

Tracey got closer and whispered, "I wish I believed that, Mr Gammon."

"Hey, you two you will be snogging next."

"Behave Shelley, good mates aren't we John?" and Tracey winked at Shelley.

It turned out to be a good night, Tracey Rodgers stayed at John's.

John still wasn't asleep at 3.15am, although Tracey was. He was thinking about Saron and how he lost her because of that stupid night, and how much heartache Anouska had caused. Then she compounded it by saying the baby was his, when in reality it was Steve's, his best mate.

John finally fell to sleep. It was 8.00am when Tracey came upstairs and woke him with a bacon sandwich and a strong black coffee.

"Thanks Trace, I could get you used to this."

"You were so restless last night, are you ok?"

"Just got a lot on at work."

"Understand that, I think most people are worried about this maniac that is

THE MEANING STONES

stalking the Peak District. I know Wez and Lindsay are worried about room bookings over the Christmas period. They said they were forty percent down on what Kev and Doreen did last year, and they can't do anything about it."

"Can see why I'm restless then."

"I certainly can. Will you drop me for my car on your way to work."

"Not a problem. I best get showered. That sandwich was lovely, thank you," and he pecked her on her cheek.

CHAPTER FOUR

Gammon arrived at work.

"Good morning, Magic."

"Morning Sir."

"Anything from last night?"

"Only some young kid caught breaking into a garden shed. The beat lads sorted it."

"Ok thanks," and Gammon climbed the stairs and grabbed a coffee. He could have sworn it was actually dishwater, it was that poor.

Gammon's desk looked like a building site, with the overflow of files and paperwork, he really hated that side of the job. Today he had decided to try and get two new Detective Inspectors; one to replace poor Danny Kiernan, and maybe another help with the current workload to replace DI Winnipeg who he hadn't replaced yet.

Gammon had almost decided earlier in the week that he could take one from Micklock. Being acting DCI over both stations he didn't have to ask. He rang Micklock and asked to speak with Detective Inspector Martin Finney and Detective Inspector Tom Stampfer, both good officers. Finney had been a DI for five years and Stampfer, the younger guy, had three years as a DI at Micklock. They both seemed genuinely excited to come and work with Gammon. Martin Finney said he lived at Dilley Dale anyway, and Tom Stampfer was hoping to move to Monkdale. Gammon said to start the next day which was Friday. His thinking was he could introduce them to the team, then Monday being the beginning of the week they would hit the ground running. He felt better he had more resources at hand, as he had a feeling this was going to be a big case. He stood looking over to Losehill

THE MEANING STONES

trying to build up some enthusiasm to start on his paperwork when his phone rang.

"DCI Gammon, can I help you?"

An Irish voce on the line began talking. "You Sir, need to be very careful where you dig, or face the consequences of your actions."

"Who is this?"

"That is the one and only warning you will get, heed what I say, DCI Gammon."

The phone went dead. Gammon tried to call it back, but the number was with-held. The chances are it was a pay as you go mobile that was in some canal now anyway.

Things like this frustrated Gammon, not the threat, he was used to that, but the cowardly way these things generally played out. It was now almost 1.15pm and he had been at the paperwork for three hours. He decided to stretch his legs and pop down and inform Magic about the new Detective Inspectors that were joining from Micklock.

He said he was to show them round the station and arrange for all staff to be at the meeting at 9.00am tomorrow so he could introduce them and get them up to speed. He could see Magic was a bit put out.

"Is there a problem, Magic?"

THE MEANING STONES

"Just I was hoping to get moved back to DS at some point Sir, and I thought this might be the time."

"Sorry Magic, not yet I'm afraid," and Gammon climbed back up the stairs. He wasn't sure if Magic was even detective material.

It was Saturday night and John had arranged to pick Tracey up to take her to the mini-bus from the Spinning Jenny to the Tow'd Man. Tracey looked stunning, she had her blonde hair put up and wore a purple dress cut just above the knee which she had matched with a short pink coat with just a cross and chain. On the way to the pub she said Steve had introduced her to her sister India, and how shocked she was that she looked so like Jo. Tracey said she thought she was a lovely girl, but felt a bit hurt she was seeing Steve. Not so much Steve, more it was her twin sister's husband.

John explained that if they were both happy, Jo would have been happy. This seemed to calm Tracey down for their arrival at the pub. They had a couple of drinks, then all piled on the bus. Tracey said Steve was meeting them there with India, and that India was her sister and

THE MEANING STONES

Jo's twin sister. Steve and India were an item. John squeezed her hand he knew how hard that had been to tell everyone. He pecked her on the cheek and whispered, "Well done."

It was a really cold night with wintry showers.

"Do you reckon we will get a white Christmas?" Carol asked.

"Bloody hell woman, give over, there is at least five weeks to Christmas," Jimmy Lowcee retorted.

The bus erupted in laughter. Good old Carol, she probably didn't know it, but she had taken the sting out of the situation for Tracey.

They walked in to the bar area and it was already full. Saron was greeting everyone as they arrived with a glass of Bucks Fizz. She looked stunning with a white sequined full length ball gown and her hair also up. John politely took a glass and tried not to make eye contact with her. He couldn't see Branch anywhere and was pleased about that. Perhaps he wasn't coming?

Steve was already there so joined the group and introduced India. Everybody was looking. It was if Jo had never been

THE MEANING STONES

taken. Steve looked so happy John thought.

They broke it to their little groups. Doreen took charge of the kitty and drinking started to ramp up. Steve stood with John. Tracey and India were talking.

"They must have so much to catch up on, Steve."

"Yes mate, Tracey was really good about it."

John didn't want to burst Steve's bubble, but he thought different. It was at that point that Sheridan Branch made his big entrance, flinging his arms round

Saron and whisking her onto the dance floor.

"Bloody hell John, who's that?"

"Sheridan Branch."

"What, from the Branch family in Ackbourne?"

"The very one."

"Is he seeing Saron then?"

"Looks like it."

"Ooh, do I detect some jealousy here Porky?"

"Leave it Steve, I'm not up for that tonight mate. Actually I could punch his lights out given half a chance, Steve."

THE MEANING STONES

"Not worth it mate, would affect your career. Now me on the other hand, it wouldn't affect me now, would it?"

"Steve, no. I fight my own battles."

Just then India and Tracey came over both wanting to dance to Wham 'Last Christmas.' The guys duly submitted. Saron was really playing up to Branch and John was feeling more aggrieved. The music stopped and as John was leaving the dance floor Saron turned to Sheridan Branch.

"Sheridan, this is John Gammon, a good friend of mine."

"Oh hey, at last I meet the famous Johnny Gammon," and he threw out his hand with a sarcastic smile on his face. It was more than John could take so he declined the hand shake and tried to walk away. Branch wasn't used to being snubbed.

"Hey Johnny Plod, do you not want to shake hands with a millionaire?" and he put his hand on John's shoulder.

Quick as a flash John turned round, hitting once in the face and on the side chopping him on his leg. He fell in a heap whimpering like a puppy. Everybody stood back in amazement and shock.

THE MEANING STONES

John walked away. He had left the pub and was halfway on the moor when Steve caught up with him.

"You silly sod, they have called for the police, John."

"I actually don't give a shit, Steve. He asked for it, the pompous prick."

They had walked almost a mile when two police cars with flashing lights pulled them over. Two young traffic cops got out of the first car.

"DCI Gammon, I'm afraid we are going to have to arrest you for the disturbance at the Tow'd Man."

John didn't resist and they took him, leaving Steve at the side of the road. He walked back with the party now ruined. The only topic of conversation was John.

"Where is he, Steve?"

"Bixton police have arrested him, Tracey."

"Oh, crap."

Saron pretended she wasn't listening, but everyone in the room knew she was. Branch was still whinging about how he would have his career. Steve wandered over and politely told him to shut his mouth, or he would finish what John started.

THE MEANING STONES

Shelley had called for the mini bus with the night ruined. Once back at the Spinning Jenny it was John who was the talking point.

"Blimey, did you see how fast he threw that punch, then buckled that bloke's leg under him."

Not a wise move thought Tracey. He will be in real trouble being a high ranking police officer.

The night had somewhat lost its interest with everyone and by11.00pm everyone had left. Steve told India he was going to go and see Saron, to see if she could get

Sheridan Branch to not press for a conviction.

"You are a nice guy, Steve," India said whilst hugging him.

"Me and John go way back, and we have been through a lot together. I will always have his back."

The following day Steve arrived at The Tow'd Man to talk with Saron. Saron's eyes were swollen, she said she had cried all night.

"You can't let Branch press charges Saron, or you know it will be the end for John's career."

"Why did he do it, Steve?"

THE MEANING STONES

"Do you really need me to tell you why? Come on Saron, you know he loves you."

"He might love me Steve, but it's not enough with these stupid things he keeps doing. I mean the other day I was told that girl he went with on our wedding eve has a child by him. He flatly denied that to me some weeks ago."

"Saron, it's not his child, it's mine."

Saron looked stunned at Steve's admission.

"What!"

"Surely you aren't going to see him lose his career? You know what that means to him."

"Steve, John is a fool to himself, we had everything. I understood his job with working in that environment, and he just blew it on some foreign tart and for what?"

Steve for once was lost for words.

"Look, I will have a word with Sheridan when I visit him today, but I am guessing he already has his solicitor lined up."

"I will call you after I have been to the hospital."

"Do your best, Saron."

"I told you, I'm not promising. I mean he broke his nose and his leg, Steve, come on it wasn't just a slap."

THE MEANING STONES

"I know that, but he was provoked. Look Saron, John is very well liked and respected in the community. If he was to lose his job because of your boyfriend, how do you think that will play out with you and your business?"

Steve could see she hadn't thought about that.

"Right, well I'm going to see him now at Bixton."

"I'll wait for your call."

Steve arrived at Bixton hoping his mate was ok. PC Magic knew Steve and with it being Sunday there wasn't many people about.

"What's happening?"

"Hello Steve, at the moment DI Smarty and DI Lee said we weren't to utter a word about this to anyone. They said they would wait and see if charges were pressed. Then they would have to inform the powers that be. So everybody is tight lipped. DI Smarty has spoken with everyone of John's staff and told them John's career is on the line if they breathed a word to the press or anyone."

"Ok, can I see him?"

"Of course."

Magic opened the cell and let Steve in.

THE MEANING STONES

"If you two want a coffee give me a shout."

"How are you mate?"

"I've been better, Steve."

"Have you heard from Saron?"

"Yes, just been to see her. I have asked her to get the scumbag to not press charges."

"What did she say?"

It was now Steve's turn to save John's feelings.

"She was going to try mate. She said she would ring me after she left the hospital."

"If he does Steve, that's my career done. The very best I will get is demotion, but they don't look favourably on a police officer attacking the public."

"What the hell made you do it?"

"I don't know. We had a couple of beers but I was fine. It was when he called me a plod in that snooty voice, I just reacted."

"Well you broke his nose and his leg, mate."

"I'm not proud of it, Steve. It's just I love her, and seeing her with that idiot I thought I could handle it, but I couldn't."

"Well, Magic told me Dave Smarty and Peter Lee are trying to keep it under wraps. Let's hope Saron comes good, John."

THE MEANING STONES

At that point Steve's phone rang. It was Saron.

"Steve, I spoke with Sheridan. He said he won't press any charges, but John has to keep away from me."

"I'm with John now, do you want to tell him?"

"No, did you not hear what I said? He won't press charges. Just tell John to keep away, Steve."

"Ok and thank you."

Saron hung up.

"Good news of sorts, John."

"What?"

"He isn't going to press charges, but only on the understanding you don't contact Saron."

"Is he serious? Bloody buffoon, who does he think he is?"

"He's the guy with your career in his hands, John. Leave it a while, I'm sure we can sort."

"Is Saron ok with it?"

"She didn't say she wasn't."

"Great blown it again."

"Look mate I best get off. I'll phone Dave Smarty and tell him then he can come and release you."

"Thanks Steve, I owe you big time."

THE MEANING STONES

"You owe me nothing, we are mates."

Smarty arrived and got John out of the cell.

"This possibly saved you career, but there were a lot of people there, and it could get back you were fighting."

"One step at a time Dave, just glad to be out. Come on I'll take you for a drink. Where do you fancy, Dave?"

"I don't know, you choose."

"Ok, let's go to Toad Holes, not been there in ages."

They arrived in the village and went into the Wobbly Man. Who was behind the bar? Only Joni.

Detective John Gammon Series Three
Book Five

"Hey, Mr Gammon."

"What you doing working here?"

"Oh, Rick got in a mess with his staff so I said I would help out."

"Anyway never mind about me. I hear our famous policeman got into a fight last night?"

"Bloody hell, who told you?"

"The jungle drums were going at 4.00am this morning. I hear you beat up Saron's new fella."

"Hardly beat him up. Anyway I don't want to talk about it. Give us two pints of Thorntree, please."

They got their drinks and sat down.

THE MEANING STONES

"Bloody hell, Dave. I didn't think word would be out that quick. I was hoping to have a few days to think about it before contacting the Chief Superintendent. In fact I think I should do that now, Dave."

"Think I agree, mate."

John rang Chief Superintendent Scott. His wife answered, and John could hear glasses clinking in the background.

"Janet Scott, may I help you?"

John took a deep breath pretty much knowing this could end his career.

"Oh yes, I'm sorry to trouble you but could I speak to Chief Superintendent Scott please?"

"Is it a police matter only we are having a dinner party?"

"Yes, I'm sorry, it is important."

"Very well," she said. "Wait a moment."

Scott came on the phone.

"This is acting DCI Gammon Sir, from Derbyshire Police."

"Well I bloody hope this is important, Gammon."

John could feel this was going downhill fast.

"I'm afraid I was involved in an altercation last night Sir, and I wanted you to be aware of it."

THE MEANING STONES

"With another officer?"

"No Sir, a member of the public."

"Bloody hell Gammon, you bloody fool."

"Are there charges to be pressed?"

"No Sir, the gentleman in question isn't pressing charges."

"Right, I will call you tomorrow," and he slammed the phone down.

"How did it go mate?" Dave asked as he sat down.

"Not good mate, he was in the middle of a dinner party, but I thought I had to get this off my chest. He is ringing me tomorrow."

"You might be ok mate, perhaps a slap on the wrist or something?"

"More likely something, Dave."

They had a couple more and Dave said he best get back. So John sat at the bar.

"Looking sorry for yourself, John."

"Been a fool, Joni."

"It's not the first time, and I bet it won't be the last."

"Oh thanks for the support."

"Look John, you have to straighten your life out. You work hard, and are successful in your career, but your private life is one long trail of disasters."

"I know, Joni."

THE MEANING STONES

"I am wondering if it's time to move on?"

"What run away, well that is really grown up, isn't it?"

She wasn't feeling sorry for John and maybe that's what he needed.

"Look I get off at 9.30pm. Have you eaten?"

"No."

"Ok, well let's try that little Chinese in the village and you can stay at mine if you want tonight. On the settee of course."

John began doing what he always did when he was in situations he didn't like, and that was drink. By the time Joni finished he was quite tipsy.

They headed down to the China Rose Garden and ate, which brought him round a little.

"Maybe I should go home?"

"No way are you driving. Are you nuts? Aren't you in enough trouble?"

They walked back up the hill to Joni's cottage.

"Hello Mr Moo-moo," she said to the ginger tom cat that made a bee-line for John.

THE MEANING STONES

Joni made two coffees and placed them on the coffee table and sat down next to John. John leaned forward to kiss her.

"Whoa, what are you doing?"

"I'm sorry, I am a bit drunk."

"You can take those ideas right out of your head, John Gammon. I am being a friend for you. Look I'm off to bed. There is a quilt cover and some sheets in that airing cupboard, and the settee pulls out to make a bed."

The following morning John felt terrible as he drove to Bixton. On arrival Magic said a Superintendent Scott was in his office with another woman who he didn't introduce. John quickly ran to the bathroom to try and straighten himself up knowing this could be the end of his career. As he climbed the stairs to his office his legs felt like jelly. He wasn't sure if that was the alcohol or the thought that this could be the end for him.

He walked in. Superintendent Scott was a tall guy in his mid-fifties with a slim grey moustache.

"John Gammon, Sir," and he went to shake Scott's hand.

"Sit down Gammon."

THE MEANING STONES

He didn't introduce the woman which John thought was odd.

"Well Gammon, you made a right bloody mess this time, and I believe looking at your record this is not an uncommon occurrence with you."

Gammon tried to butt in. Scott was having none of it.

"I should bloody throw you off the force, but the one thing going for you is your ability. You are a good copper, albeit a stupid one at times. This is what is going to happen, but this is totally dependent on no charges being pressed against you. You are suspended for three days as of now.

You are also no longer acting DCI. You are just a Detective Inspector, and this is the new DCI here at Bixton, DCI Heather Burns. I expect you to be professional and help Heather all the way. Think of yourself as a very lucky man. That's me done. Take the garden leave Gammon and let's hope there are no repercussions."

"Thank you, Heather, I will be in touch."

He scowled at Gammon as he left.

"Well John, I guess nobody wanted this to happen. I know very little about you so before you go off shall we have a coffee somewhere? Then on my return I will tell the team the situation."

Gammon agreed feeling relieved it was now out in the open as long as idiot kept his word and didn't press charges.

"Follow me Heather, I will take you to a little café. It's a small walk from a pub carpark but a beautiful walk if you like walking."

"Love walking John, living in Scotland in the Highlands you would be mad not to enjoy walking."

John pulled into the car park at Up the Steps Maggie's and showed Heather down the steps into Monkdale, and the short walk to the Sloppy Quiche Café. Jimmy was cooking so a young girl took their order of two toasted tea cakes and two coffees.

"So you decked a member of the public, can I ask why?"

"It's a bit embarrassing. He is seeing a woman I was going to marry last Christmas. We were at a pre-Christmas party and he smirked at me and called me plod. I just saw red, broke his nose and his leg."

"What and he isn't pressing charges?"

"No."

"Why?"

THE MEANING STONES

"On the condition I don't go anywhere near Saron, the girl in question."

"How come you didn't get married last Christmas?"

"It's a long story Heather. Anyway, where are you staying?"

"I'm going to look for somewhere after this, why do you know somewhere?"

"I know a lovely place, I'll give Lisa a ring if you wish."

"Great John, thank you."

"It's a gorgeous place, real five star and Lisa and Jim can't do enough for you, Heather. It's called Cambridge Lodge just

down the road from Swinster at Clough
Dale."

John rang, and as usual Lisa was very
efficient.

"Hi Lisa, John Gammon. I wondered if
Cambridge Lodge is free for a few weeks
for a colleague."

"Blimey John, that's what I call timing.
A bloke just had to cancel. He was
working at Pippa's Frozen Foods, but his
wife has been taken ill. He won't be back
for minimum five weeks his company
said. So yes, I have. Is it a gentleman or a
lady?"

THE MEANING STONES

"It's a lady Lisa, her name is Heather Burns. We will be with you in about forty minutes, if that's ok?"

"Brilliant John thanks for thinking of us."

John and Heather finished their breakfast and headed back down Monkdale to the well-worn stone steps leading up to the pub car park.

"This is a lovely place, it's like Scotland, John."

"Yes, it does remind me of Scotland. Home from home, Heather."

"Really appreciate your help."

"I've nothing else to do. I'm on garden leave remember," and they both smiled.

John set off with Heather following him. He thought Heather was about in her mid-thirties with jet black hair and very pretty eyes and teeth. She was one of those people that when she smiled it like enveloped you and made you feel good. He was thinking that maybe just being a DI was better anyway. He hated the paperwork and the politics, catching baddies was what he enjoyed.

They arrived at Lisa's and John left Heather looking round Cambridge Lodge which he knew she would be super

THE MEANING STONES

impressed with. He decided to go home, put on his Rab coat and walking boots, and do a good walk. It was ages since he had done that.

He set off from his cottage and walked about two miles before eventually getting close to Sheba Filey's cottage. The cottage with its walled garden was a gem, and as he walked past the gate he saw Sheba. She waved and came down the path.

"Hiya John, how are you? Off on a walk?"

"Yeah, ages since I have done a few miles."

"Do you want a coffee and a slice of my lemon drizzle cake?"

"Too good to turn down that, Sheba."

He followed her back up the yard. Sheba was a very pretty girl, and even in her cow muck wellies she still looked amazing.

The farm house was neat and tidy with the obligatory large farmhouse table where the lemon drizzle cake sat proudly waiting to be consumed. Sheba made two coffees and sat with John, both armed with a piece of cake.

"So how's life treating Sheba?"

"Oh, not bad John, me and Phil called it a day, it just wasn't working."

THE MEANING STONES

"Sorry to hear that."

"What is this I hear? You were fighting at the Tow'd Man, something to do with Saron's latest beau," and she laughed.

"Wasn't exactly a fight, hence me walking today. I have been put on garden leave for the three days, and had the acting DCI position taken off me."

"Oh John, I am sorry."

"Well could have been worse. I could have lost my job, so I am thankful for small mercies. The guy she is seeing is a total prat, always has been. He is just a little rich kid. She is just another trophy for him to go with his flash cars and big house."

"Well, I still shouldn't have broken his nose and leg. I am supposed to uphold the law."

"Well different folk that have spoken to me support you. They all think he is a dick, John. Look, don't think I am being inhospitable, but got loads to do on the farm. Call me if you fancy a beer one night."

"I'll take you up on that," and John set off walking towards Custard Fields. He arrived at the top then headed along the old railway track before following the

THE MEANING STONES

valley down into Monkdale. He passed the Sloppy Quiche Café, probably the first time in his life he hadn't called. The lemon drizzle cake needed walking off John thought. He then climbed out of Monkdale and headed towards Dumpling Dale. Dumpling Dale apparently got its name from Sir John De Ling. But during time it became Dumpling Dale nobody knows why.

John finally arrived in the village of Pommie. It was now almost 3.00pm. Luckily the little village bakery and café was still open. The lady said she would have normally been shut, but they are busy making Christmas Cakes to order so she kept it open.

John ordered a sausage roll with a salad and a strong black coffee. Once finished he paid his bill and headed back to Hittington, which he estimated would take about three hours if he got a spurt on. Part of the return home involved a small stretch of road which he didn't like, not that it was busy, just it was a road. It was only about a quarter of a mile, then he headed into the next field. In the distance he could see a person who he assumed was sitting having a coffee and a sandwich. But as he got closer he could see the person was

THE MEANING STONES

propped up against a large stone. John realised it was another victim. The woman had two dice in her eyes both showing number four and there was one of her eyes on the stone. The body was at the back of the stone. On the front was some old lettering carved in it.

'Life is value. Value is knowing your sins. Stay now and reflect on your life then leave me here alone knowing you leave me a better person'

John ran back to the road to get a signal. He called Bixton so that Magic could get Wally, his team and DS Bass and DI Milton. He also quickly spoke with DCI

Burns who told him she had explained the situation. She said she was coming out too.

John went back to the victim, not that he could do anything for her. He thought the body had been out in the elements for a few days.

The team finally arrived, and DCI Burns took charge.

"Never out of the bloody limelight, are you John? Can you imagine the headlines in the next issue of the local paper?"

"Just my luck Ma'am."

Heather Burns laughed.

THE MEANING STONES

"Well you better get your backside in work tomorrow. I'm not having my best office swanning round the country looking for bodies. I'll see you in the morning meeting assuming John Walvin has something for us at 9.00am, John."

"He will have, he is a diamond, Ma'am."

John set off walking and arrived back at 7.40pm. He showered changed and drove to the Spinning Jenny.

"Hi John."

"How are you, Wez?"

"Yeah, not bad mate. I hear things didn't go to well at the Tow'd Man the other night."

"Let's just forget it mate."

"Oh yeah sorry, I bet everybody is talking about it."

"Pint of Pedigree please, Wez."

John cut him short, it was getting tiresome everybody commenting.

There was nobody in who John knew so he sat by the fire thinking. Suddenly the door opened and Donna and Saron appeared. She couldn't see John from the bar. They were both clearly a bit drunk.

"Are you Wez?"

THE MEANING STONES

"Yes."

"I'm Saron and this is Donna. We are co-owners of the Tow'd Man. We are having our Christmas party now before the rush."

"Pleased to meet you. Have you been far?"

"Had a meal in Toad Holes, and a couple of bottles of wine. I think we best get a taxi from here though."

"Good idea, girls."

Then Donna spotted John.

"Saron, John is by the fire."

She wandered over platting her legs as she went.

"Hey, what you doing Mr Lonesome?" she said slurring her speech.

"Oh, just having a quite drink gathering my thoughts."

"Are you going to give me and Donna a lift home?"

"If you need one. Let me finish this and I will shout you."

Saron staggered back to tell Donna they were having a lift back.

"Are you sure about this, Saron?"

"Yeah, what's his face is in hospital."

Donna took charge of the situation and went over to John.

THE MEANING STONES

"Look John, if you don't mind giving us a lift back to the Tow'd Man that's great. But I don't want that dick head finding out and you losing your job. You wait in the car-park and I will bring her out. That way nobody knows."

John did as instructed. Eventually they came out. Saron was singing in the car all the way back. Donna left John with her. He said he would put her to bed. He carried her upstairs in her apartment and lay her on the bed.

"I will undress you, but need the toilet first."

When he came back to the bedroom
Saron had undressed down to her white
basque. She had such a terrific figure. Her
blonde hair fell seductively over her milky
white shoulders.

"Make love to me, John," she pouted.

Now it was dilemma time; career or
Saron. There was only ever going to be
one winner in that two horse race. He
quickly stripped off and lay on top of her,
first kissing her neck which he knew sent
her wild, before working his way down
her fantastic body. John then held her
tightly as she ravished him. Saron was

insatiable. They made love before both collapsing in total fulfilment.

"I love you John but, I can't be with you," she said before laying her head on his chest and falling asleep. John lay there in pure ecstasy with his Saron before falling asleep.

CHAPTER FIVE

The following morning Saron said she had a hangover.

"What about last night?"

"Look John, I told you I am not worth losing your career for. What's done is done. Please go bcforc you are spotted and it gets back to him."

John left feeling even more confused. There had to be a way round this. He arrived at work just before the meeting was to start. When he walked in the incident room they all clapped. Gammon felt quite humble. DCI burns stood up.

THE MEANING STONES

"Thank you everybody for a great reception to DI Gammon, who is and will always be a valued member of this team. Having said that, John you are leading this case and unluckily for you yesterday you found the latest victim."

Gammon came to the front.

"First of all, thank you so much for your support in what was a stupid act on my part. Secondly, we have a new DCI, Heather Burns, who I believe will be a massive plus for Bixton and Derbyshire police. Ok, yesterday I found what I believe was the third victim. So as usual Wally what have you got for us?"

"Ok, well the victim is a Marilyn Wilson. She was approximately thirty eight years old. I believe she was murdered possibly between six or eight days ago. Like the other victims her eyes had been gouged out and replaced with two dice, one in each eye socket. This time two fours were pointing forward. Whoever is doing this I believe wants six victims and now we have three."

"Ok Wally, thanks."

"DS Bass, can you get an address for Marilyn Wilson, then give me a shout and we will let her family know. I'm assuming this lady has not been reported missing?"

THE MEANING STONES

"No Sir, I checked that."

"Ok, well let's get today out of the way then we can meet same time tomorrow and see where we are at, if that's ok, DCI Burns?"

"Yes that's fine John. 9.00am tomorrow then everybody."

Gammon went back to his office to clear his paperwork up while he waited for DS Bass. He stood looking out of his window. What could the connection between these Meaning Stones and the dice? There must be a connection John thought. He also could not get Saron out of his mind. Was this because she was playing him? Only

Lyndsay had done that before. He had been determined not to let another woman do that to him, and now he was feeling the same with Saron.

There was a knock on his office door DS Bass popped her head round.

"I have an address for Marilyn Wilson."

"Ok where is it, Kate."

"Would you believe she lives at Katherine's Cottage, Ardwalk. My nanna always called me Katherine, bless her."

"Ok, well grab your coat we best go and do this."

The drive to Ardwalk was especially nice. It was a cold but crisp day and the

THE MEANING STONES

sun had hardly come up so the fields leading to Ardwalk all had a heavy frost on them.

"Oh, I love this time of year, Sir. I am so looking forward to Christmas. Have you got much planned?"

"Not really Kate, I'm afraid I have no family now. Well to be honest that isn't strictly true. I have a half -sister but she is all over the world, so I don't see much of her."

"Oh dear, that's sad. Where will you have Christmas dinner?"

"I'm not sure yet. I'll find somewhere."

Ardwalk was a cluster of what had been small farms and a pub which was now a house, although a new brewery had just opened up. Katherine's house was right across from where you drove into the small hamlet.

Gammon and Bass opened the small wooden green painted gate and walked up the small path leading to a stable door. Gammon knocked on the door. He tried several times but there was no answer.

"Come on Kate, I have a couple of friends that live just over there. Shelley and Jack Etchings, they may be able to help us.

THE MEANING STONES

Shelley and Jack had a beautiful barn conversion and a five star farmhouse they rented out called Town Head Farm. Shelley was booked up year in year out. As they walked across the cobbled courtyard Shelley was just coming out of the holiday accommodation.

"Hello John, to what do we hold this pleasure for? I'm not in trouble, am I?"

Shelley was good, she didn't ask about his trouble with having DS Bass with him.

"No Shelley, we are looking for a Mr Wilson who lives at Katherine's Cottage."

"Andy? Nice guy, him and his wife. He works away on the oil rigs and she does something from home. Funnily enough John, I haven't seen Marilyn for a couple of days, but then again she is always walking somewhere. Hey, you are in luck, that's Andy there getting out of that taxi. He must be home for a few weeks."

Shelley waved at Andy and he waved back.

"Thanks Shelley, we best go and see him."

Gammon and DS Bass strode over to Katherine's Cottage just as he was about to close the door.

THE MEANING STONES

"Mr Wilson?" Gammon said flashing his warrant card. "DI Gammon and DS Bass, may we come in?"

Andy was flustered. He got inside and shouted, "Marilyn, Marilyn I'm home. We have two policemen here."

"I'm afraid Mrs Wilson won't answer Sir. She was found murdered near Pommie a couple of days ago."

"No, not my Marilyn."

"Please Sir, sit down."

"DS Bass, get Mr Wilson a glass of water please."

Andy Wilson tried to gather himself and very quickly realised this was for real.

"Why would somebody hurt my Marilyn? She was such a gentle person, Mr Gammon."

"That is what we intend to find out. Would you be ok to answer a few questions? I will keep it as brief as possible."

Wilson nodded.

"How long have you lived in Ardwalk?"

"About eighteen months."

"And where was home before that?"

"We lived in London because of Marilyn's job. You see I can live anywhere with my job because I am away for long lengths of time. We chose the

THE MEANING STONES

Peak District because Marilyn loves walking. She would quite often bring herself up here for long weekends while I was away. She stayed at Shelley's, that's how we got to hear about Katherine's Cottage coming up for sale. It was two strokes of luck. Marilyn had applied to a company here in Derbyshire. She does some kind of rules to do with gambling. Her previous job was working at a big casino in London, but she got so fed up of London she took less money and we moved here. We have no children so it was quite seamless, although her boss at the casino wasn't happy."

"Do you have a name for her boss."

"Yes, it was Mr Lomax."

Gammon looked at DS Bass as she was taking notes.

"You don't think he had anything to do with this, do you Mr Gammon?"

"We never rule anybody out Mr Wilson, not until the perpetrator is found. But to be honest, unless Mr Lomax has found some way of reincarnation it's doubtful, as he is also no longer with us."

"Oh, Marilyn never said but last three months we have hardly any internet or Skype due to weather conditions, so communication has been poor."

THE MEANING STONES

"Do you need some grief counselling Mr Wilson, or somebody to sit with you?"

"No, I will go and see Shelley and Jack."

"I am going to have to ask you to officially identify Marilyn, I'm afraid."

"Ok, Mr Gammon."

"If you could be at the station for 11.00am and ask for John Walvin."

"Ok, Mr Gammon."

Gammon and Bass got back in the car.

"Poor man, Sir."

"Yes, he took it well, sad time for him I guess."

Detective John Gammon Series Three
Book Five

Gammon and bass arrived back at almost lunchtime and he went straight to see DCI Burns.

"Oh John, just the man, I see paperwork isn't your favourite past time John."

"You guessed right there, Ma'am."

"Please John, when there are no other officers about it's Heather."

"Ok Heather."

"I think we should have a catch up with the team after lunch, and it will help me as well."

"Sounds good."

"Shall I say 2pm?"

"Ok, that's good for me."

THE MEANING STONES

"How did you get on with Mr Wilson?"

"He had just arrived back from working on the oil rigs. Poor guy, must have been a hell of a blow."

"Yes, I can't imagine, John."

Just then John's phone rang and it was Fleur.

"Sorry Heather, do you mind if I take this?"

"Not a problem John. See you in the incident room at 2.00pm. I'll let the others know."

"Ok, thanks Heather."

"Hi Fleur, this is a surprise."

"Can you talk, John?"

"Yes why?"

"I have just heard about your demotion."

"How did you hear about that?"

"A colleague was lifting a file about bloody Brian Lund and your name came up."

"Why?"

"Well, it gets worse. The guy you hit was a known associate of Brian Lund, and he has friends in high places, John. You don't do things in half measures, do you?"

"What did it say?"

THE MEANING STONES

"Look, I don't have long but I am hoping to come to you for Christmas."

"Oh brilliant Fleur, let me know for sure soon though."

"It would be better if we spoke then, not on the phone."

"Ok, can't wait to see you."

Fleur hung up. That's Christmas sorted he hoped.

It was almost 2.00pm so John headed down to the incident room.

"Ok thanks everybody, I thought it would be a good idea to pool what we have, and it will also get me up to speed on the case. So if you don't mind John."

John pointed to the three victims.

"We have number one, Anthony Smidge, or that's what his alias was. He was actually Leslie Brough, one time hit man for Johnny Guitar Lomax, now deceased, but apparently not a man to cross when he was alive. Brough stole off Lomax, disappeared from London, and came to stay with us here in the Peak District. He brought with him a former madam, Marilyn Kaiser. She also knew Lomax after some time they split. Before he was murdered he bought Kaiser a small café in Swinster. To me it was if he was getting his house in order, so did he know

THE MEANING STONES

his killer? A certain Gary Birch had a grudge against Leslie Brough. He was with him the day he took the money. Little Gary Birch, as he was known, became Lomax's new hit man replacing Brough. A couple of days ago DS Bass and DI Smarty went to London to question him. He had a full blown alibi for the date of the killing. My money is still on him, he will have bought the alibi for sure. Brough was found at Magpie Mine near Shealdon. He was propped against a war memorial for three men Walter Plantager, Thomas Myers and Harry Salt. Salt's grandson also called Harry Salt is an interesting one. He works for the gaming commission but has a liking for the ladies, so is clearly open to the underworld. We need to watch this guy closely."

"Victim number two, Robert Bloom, ex-casino owner with his partner Harbey Clayton. Bloom got Lomax's daughter pregnant. Him and Harbey did time for evading tax before leaving London and coming to live in Swinster. Also bit of a co-incidence in that Kaiser now lives in Swinster, with the café which Brough bought for her with the money he stole from Lomax. Bloom was found just like Brough with his eyes gouged out and

THE MEANING STONES

replaced with two dice set at number five. Brough was set at six. Both men had one eye taken and one left at the scene."

"The Meaning Stone, as they are called in these parts, where Robert Bloom was propped up against said,

'Take a while to sit and view
The wonders of nature given but not due
Take your time and sit a while
For life will leave you without a smile
Your time will come but oh so quick
And leave a memory made of stick
The stick will break and so will you
So enjoy now my friend for life is not
just for you'."

"Our third victim was a lady called Mary Wilson from Ardwalk. I found her whilst out walking."

"On your garden leave, Sir."

"Yes thank you, DS Yap."

"She was also propped up against a Meaning Stone with both eyes gouged out, and two dice both set at the number four. I have since found out she was also from London and also worked for Lomax before swapping jobs and coming to live here in the Peak District."

"So we have a killer that appears to be killing anybody that has had an association with Johnny Guitar Lomax. Why are they

THE MEANING STONES

left propped against Meaning Stones? As it stands we only have Gary Birch as our suspect, and he has worked himself an alibi."

"DS Bass, take DI Milton and let's dig real deep into Harry Salt. I want to know everything about this guy, and all his indiscretions."

"Ok, unless DCI Burns has any questions that's it from me."

"Thank you, John."

"I just want to say we are heading to a Christmas break and we really don't want this hanging over us. I am sure you are doing your best, but this area relies heavily on tourism. If people are scared to go walking in the Peak District they will go somewhere else, and we can't let that happen to the community. Thank you."

They all left and Burns asked John to stay a minute.

"I got a call yesterday from a newspaper, the Micklock Mercury, they want to come and see me. Anything I should be aware of John?"

"I would think it would be Billy Hutchinson. Do you want me to attend?"

"No, I will be fine John, but thank you."

Gammon went back to his office and decided to try and get some dirt on Saron's

THE MEANING STONES

boyfriend with what Fleur had said about the Brian Lund file she had seen.

The other thing bothering John was whoever killed Daniel Kiernan was still loose. This must tie up with the serial killer with DS Bass saying he had gone out early morning working on a lead.

John stood in his favourite spot in his office looking towards Losehill. If he could get something on Sheridan Branch. He knew that someday this guy was going to want something for his silence, plus he couldn't see Saron. It was not only great to have Fleur, because now he had some family. It was also great what she knew, and this looked like it could be another scrape she may get him out of.

He was thinking about Saron. He always bought her a present at Christmas, but this year could be tricky with 'idiot brain' about. The Peak District had quite a few festivals on the run up to Christmas. One of John's favourites was the trip to Castleting, an old village that had stood for centuries. It even had a castle built in the 10th Century for one of William the Conqueror's illegitimate children. The ruins still stood majestically on the hill overlooking the village. Each shop had a Christmas tree and from 6.30pm every

THE MEANING STONES

night Carol Singers walked the streets stopping at strategic place to sing carols. People sold horse-chestnuts from braziers It was how most people saw a Dickensian Christmas.

It's funny how deja-vu happens. His phone rang, and it was Sheba.

"Hey John, they are having a trip from the Spinning Jenny to Castleting this Saturday and I wondered if you fancied going?"

"Hey, that would be great, if you pay I will sort mine and yours out. What time are they going?"

"5.30pm. Apparently Wez and Lindsay have managed to fill a forty two seater bus this year."

"Wow, should be a good night then."

"Guess so, John. Do you want me to pick you up?"

"No, I can meet you at the Spinning Jenny at 5.00pm then we can have a quick drink before we get on the bus."

"Sounds like a plan, look forward to it Sheba."

John felt quite pleased Sheba rang, they had always been quite close. He always liked the Castleting trip in kind of set you up for Christmas a favourite time for John.

THE MEANING STONES

Going on his own really would not have been an option.

Gammon's phone rang.

"DI Gammon, can you come through I have Mr Hutchinson in my office, and I think it only fair you hear what he has to say."

Heather Burns seemed quite formal and She hadn't seemed like that up until now.

Gammon knocked on DCI Burns's office door. He seemed to have been a frequent visitor to this office over the years. Burns shouted him to enter. She was sitting behind her desk and the little weasel that is Billy Hutchinson was on a chair in front of the desk. He leaned forward offering his hand in a welcome gesture. Gammon ignored him and instead he looked at Burns.

"How can I help you, Ma'am?"

"Take a seat, DI Gammon."

"Please Mr Hutchinson, tell Mr Gammon what you are stating you are going to write in your paper for the Saturday edition."

"Well I have known Mr Gammon for many years and my editor thought it only fair he had a chance to comment without prejudice about the article."

THE MEANING STONES

"The headline will be 'High ranking police officer Gammon is demoted after fracas with local business man Sheridan Branch'. The article will tell how you broke his nose and his leg, how the Branch family have always been very supportive to local charities, how well liked Sheridan is and how this is yet another case of police brutality."

"Obviously we will pad it out, so I wondered if you have any comment to make, Mr Gammon."

"Hutchinson, I have no comment to make."

"Do you need anything more from me, Ma'am?"

"Thank you, John."

Hutchinson was in her office for another thirty minutes before he left. Then Burns came to Gammon's office.

"He is a bloody weasel, Heather."

"Calm down John, the story won't run."

"How have you managed that?"

"I have told him once we catch this serial killer, I will inform him before the nationals get a sniff."

"Thank you, Ma'am."

"Not just a pretty face," she said as she turned to leave.

THE MEANING STONES

"Heather, before you leave. I can't tell you where I got this, but I have been told on good authority that Sheriadan Branch is involved with the Lund gang."

"Really? I read up on that. Wasn't the leader Brian Lund found dead?"

"Best thing that ever happened to Derbyshire, Heather."

"So you think Branch is involved in what?"

"Unsure yet, but quite possibly drugs, prostitution, illegal immigrants."

"Wow, that would be a nice little result."

"I was going to ask you if I could have round the clock surveillance on Branch now he is out of hospital?"

"Take what you need John, this could get this monkey off your back once and for all."

"Ok, I will get DI Smarty and DS Yap to run the surveillance, Heather."

"Just keep me up to speed, John."

Gammon felt good as DCI Burns left. She seemed different to the other DCIs they had before at Bixton, so he hoped things wouldn't change. Gammon spoke with DI Smarty and he was going to do

THE MEANING STONES

8.00am-8.00pm and Yap was doing the night shift.

A couple of days passed, and Gammon was driving in to work taking the scenic route when he got a call from DI Smarty.

"John, last night at 6.10pm a blue Mercedes came to Yadkin Manor. It stayed for about fifteen minutes, then I saw Branch come out and get in the vehicle. They drove to the Drovers Arms. They were in there about fifteen minutes then Branch came out with the heavy and two girls. The heavy drove the vehicle and the girls and Branch got in the back. He had a large green holdall with him. They arrived back and then I handed over to Yap."

DS Yap said the Mercedes and the people he had described had not left Yadkin Manor as yet.

"Ok, good work Dave, I'll wait to hear from DS Yap. Sounds like this guy isn't what everyone thinks he is. Gammon's dilemma was Saron. Did he tell her? She had been in the police force so knew the protocol. He decided to leave it until something concrete had been found on Branch. He arrived at work to be met by PC Magic.

THE MEANING STONES

"Sir, I have a Philip Hutch waiting in room one. He said he needed to speak with you."

"Ok then I best see him, Magic."

John went in.

"John, long time no see," said the guy who looked sixty years old. Gammon had not got a clue who he was.

"You don't remember me, do you?"

"Sorry Mr Hutch, I don't."

"I'm Pip, remember you and Steve Lineman used to call me Pip out of Great Expectations."

"Wow Pip, I didn't recognise the name. You were Philip Sloe in those days."

"Yeah, my Mum and Dad split up and we moved to Scotland to be near Mum's family. Anyway she remarried a guy called Jack Hutch. I was only eleven, so they changed my surname to Hutch."

Gammon was thinking this is all good but what did Pip want?

"Anyway mate, that copper that was killed. I think I saw who did it, well certainly the car. It was a grey Astra I didn't get all the number plate, but I think it was UN** S*L. Pretty sure the last letter was an L. It was a foggy night; the car had stopped and I assumed he had hit a badger or something, so I didn't stop."

THE MEANING STONES

"Why didn't you come forward sooner, Pip?"

"To be honest John, I really didn't think much of it. I had been at work at Obney Cement works. I bag up between 8.00pm and 4.00am, and I was tired and needed to get home. It was only when I saw an old newspaper at work in the canteen, and it said a young copper was found with all these injuries that I put two and two together."

"Well thanks Pip, at least we may find how young Kiernan died. Just write down your address, you may be needed as a witness."

"There you go, John."

"I haven't seen Lineman. I heard he went in the Navy. I only came back two months back and live in Alford in the Water, so don't see any of the old crew."

"No, Steve is about, he came out of the Navy."

"What does he do now then?"

"Bit of everything, you know Steve."

"Yeah, even as a young lad he could duck and dive, hey John."

John remembered why they called him Pip as he left. It wasn't because of his name and the character from Great Expectations. They called him Pip squeak because he was small and was always telling tales to the teachers.

Gammon called DI Milton and DS Bass to his office.

"First of all, what have you got for me on Harry Salt?"

"Quite a bit, Sir. His phone records show he calls a number at least three times a week. Her name is Katarina Kosh and she has had two convictions for prostitution. She is also a known associate of Gary Birch, by that I mean it appears he now runs her."

"Great work, Bass."

"Not all me Sir, Carl found the connection to Birch."

"Ok Carl, you get on to Scotland Yard. I want you down there to interview her ASAP."

"DS Bass, I have another one for you. We may have a witness to the demise of Daniel Kiernan. I have a number plate, well partial, which is UN something, something then a gap, then S, something, L. I need this vehicle finding Kate. It's a grey Astra."

"Not a problem, Sir."

"Carl, let me know as soon as you have to leave."

THE MEANING STONES

Gammon went straight to DCI Burns and gave her an update which seemed positive for once.

Gammon was still unsure whether to get a present for Saron. He decided to go into Bixton, to a little jeweller who specialised in special jewellery. He left work at 5.00pm. DI Milton had left for London. DS Bass was still trying to find the elusive Astra.

John parked in the precinct which was free to Christmas Shoppers in December and he headed to Goddard's jewellers.

"Good evening Sir," the elderly gentleman said. "How may I be of assistances tonight?"

"Well I want a piece of jewellery, a bracelet making, but I need it for this Saturday."

"I'm sorry Sir, I don't think that is possible. But may I show you what we have."

"You can do, but it was specific, and I wanted it engraving."

"The engraving would not be a problem."

The old guy showed John a selection of bracelets, and he couldn't believe his luck,

THE MEANING STONES

the exact one he wanted was there. John pointed to it.

"This one, Sir?"

He laid it on a purple velvet cushion.

"This is a silver bracelet with five stones, an emerald and a sapphire each side of a two carat pink diamond. This very rare diamond Sir, which reflects the price."

"What is the price?"

The old guy turned over the small label.

"It's twenty six thousand, seven hundred, Sir."

"I'll take it. Could you engrave it?"

"Of course Sir, I can have this ready for Friday if you call at the same time."

John wrote a cheque and gave him the words he wanted engraving. *'You will search for me in another person but you will never find me'.*

"Thank you, Sir, we will see you on Friday evening."

John left the shop happy with his purchase but apprehensive about giving it to Saron. He was hoping she would be on the Castleting trip.

John left with a somewhat lighter bank balance, but he knew he had to prove to

THE MEANING STONES

her what he thought. She wasn't materialistic, but she was honest, and John hadn't been always with her.

He decided to call and see Wez. Just by chance Kev was in. He said it was his domino night.

"Are you going Saturday to Castleting?"

"Never missed before mate."

"I just wondered with you not being with Saron, and I am guessing the new guy will be on the trip."

"Promise I will keep my hands in my pockets."

"You need to lad, or you will lose everything you ever worked for, and that prat will win as those kind of people always do."

Kev was like a dad to John and he could share anything with him, and he knew it would go no further.

"Look Kev, between me and you, I may have a lead on old fancy pants. He is pretty much holding me to ransom at the minute. He won't press charges as long as I keep away from Saron. Could you do me a favour on Saturday?"

"If I can lad."

"Can you get him away from her for about five minutes?"

"You aren't going to see her, are you?"

THE MEANING STONES

"Just leave that with me, I will give you the nod when I am ready."

"Who are you taking on Saturday?"

"Sheba Filey."

"I thought she was with Phil Sterndale."

"No, they split, he is with a lady called Linda now."

"Blimey, there's me and Doreen been together forty odd years and never a cross word."

John almost choked on his beer.

"In your dreams old mate."

"What I meant was, you young ones change your women like I change my underpants," and he chuckled like only Kev could.

"John, just be careful, Sheba is a lovely girl."

"Hey Kev, I know that, she is also a good mate of mine, so I am not going to do anything to hurt her, I promise."

"Ok, what you drinking John? Not that I should ask, I should know."

"Pedigree, I guess."

"Well surprise, surprise, Mr Policeman."

John stuck it until 10.00pm with Kev playing dominoes, and he had roped Wez in as well. He called it a night and

THE MEANING STONES

headed home.

Gammon arrived at work the next day and almost immediately DS Bass was knocking on his office door.

"I think I found the car, Sir."

"Ok Kate, who owns it?"

"It's registered to a Diane McGhee from Rowksly."

"Have you got an address?"

"Yes, 15 Station Terrace, Sir."

"Ok, grab your coat DS Bass, let's pay Diane McGhee a visit."

Gammon and Bass arrived at the address and the grey Astra was parked outside.

Gammon looked at the driver's side wing before going to the house. Somebody had attempted to pull a big dent out of the wing, and it had also been sprayed but quite badly.

"Well done Kate, I think we have the car. Now let's go and see what she has to say for herself, shall we?"

Gammon knocked on what had been railway cottages for the men that worked on the railway before the Beeching cuts had decimated the village by closing the railway.

THE MEANING STONES

They knocked four times before a man answered the door. Gammon and Bass showed their warrant cards.

"We wish to speak with Diane McGhee, is she in?"

"Di," shouted the scruffy looking guy. He had black jogging bottoms and a white vest covered in food stains.

"The coppers are here to speak with you."

A woman in her mid-forties and quite overweight came to the door.

"How can I help you?"

"Is that your Grey Astra on the road side there?"

"Yes, why?"

"We believe it was involved in a hit and run some days ago which killed a police officer."

"What are you talking about? I haven't driven it for the last six months. I got a drink driving ban."

"Is anybody else insured to drive it?"

"Brian," she hollered, and the guy came back.

"You drove my Astra?"

"Why?"

"Because it was involved in an accident."

THE MEANING STONES

The guy stood for a second then started giving out excuses.

"Mr McGhee, I would like you to come to the station, we need to talk."

"Take him to the car, DS Bass."

They left Station Terrace with Diane McGhee shouting obscenities, first at her husband, then at Gammon, but he just carried on. They arrived back at the station and Gammon offered him a call to get a solicitor. He declined. Gammon then offered a duty solicitor, he declined again.

"Ok Mr McGhee, or may I call you Brian?"

He nodded to say that was ok. The man smelt heavily of tobacco and sweat. It was making Gammon and Bass feel like being sick. Bass switched on the tape and gave the necessary introductions.

"Ok Brian, have you driven the Grey Astra that is registered with DVLA in Diane McGhee's name?"

"Yes?"

"Are you registered with her insurance or your own?"

He hesitated.

"Look, I needed to get to work and she had gone to see her sister, so I took it."

THE MEANING STONES

"Do you admit to having the accident close to Obney Cement Works and near the Jug Hare public house?"

Again McGhee hesitated.

"I didn't see him, it was foggy."

"So where had you been?"

"At the Jug Hare, we were having a bit of a session. It was early morning and this guy came from nowhere. Next thing I heard a bump and I had hit him. I had somehow mounted his body with my wheel. I got out and I panicked. I reversed and pulled off. I could just see him getting up, so I thought he was going to be ok."

"Look, I was frightened. I had no insurance, driving a car that wasn't mine, and I had been drinking. What was I supposed to do?"

Gammon at this point almost lost it. He called DI Lee in to take a statement. He told Kate to leave for the night as she was physically upset, and he wasn't feeling much better. He climbed the stairs to tell DCI Burns about the arrest. She was pleased but still Gammon wasn't happy.

"Why was he there Heather? He had to have known something as he implied so to Kate Bass."

THE MEANING STONES

"John, let's take the positives. We have got DI Kiernan's killer and that's all that matters."

"I suppose so Heather. Let's hope Dave Smarty has the same luck down in London."

"Could just be our day, John. Do you want me to call his parents?"

"Would you mind, Heather?"

"No problem, John."

Gammon left her office feeling pleased that they had one killer in the bag, but still mindful Kiernan had been there for a reason.

It then came to him. I bet nobody checked Danny's phone. He called DS Bass.

"Kate, was a phone found in Danny's possessions."

"No, I don't think so. I will check with Wally."

"Speak later, Kate."

Gammon rushed down to Wally.

"Did Danny Kiernan have a phone on him when you checked him out?"

"Yes, I gave it to Magic for his parents to sign for it."

"Brilliant, thanks Wally."

THE MEANING STONES

Gammon went back to his office and rang Mrs Kiernan.

"Oh hello, this is John Gammon from Bixton Police."

"Oh hello, we have just had Heather Burns on to tell us the good news."

"Yes, I just wondered if you still had Daniel's phone?"

"Yes I do Mr Gammon, but it wasn't charged when your Mr Magic gave it to me to sign for."

"Could I ask you to charge it, and I will be down to see you in the morning to explain?"

"Yes I will, Mr Gammon."

John thanked her and hung up. He nipped next and told Heather Burns where he was going tomorrow.

"There may be a chance he had somebody's number who may have tipped him off, and that's why he was where he was Heather."

"It's a long shot John, but we have nothing to lose."

"Ok, well I guess I will be back around lunchtime tomorrow, Heather."

Gammon headed back to his office and took a call from DI Milton.

"I have interviewed Katarina Kosh. This is one frightened woman, John. She

THE MEANING STONES

initially refused to talk but slowly I got things out of her. She runs three girls and herself in a house in Putney, all supplied by Gary Birch. She said the three girls are all illegal immigrants, one is from Poland and the other two a Latvian. She said Birch has a minder at the house full time. They are only allowed out if another guy comes with them. She said he would kill her if he finds out she talked. I asked her about Harry Salt. She said she knew him as Steve Digby. She said he worked in IT at a bank in the city, but she said she knew it was rubbish, because she saw him one night on the TV, and he works for the Gaming Commission."

"She said she knew a lot about him. She said he can be very nasty unless she does as he tells her. She said he comes round three nights a week and pays her one hundred and fifteen pounds a night, or at least he did. She said Gary Birch had told her there was no charge to Mr Digby anymore, as they had an arrangement and she was to keep him sweet."

"I think we need to get these girls out of this John, or we can't take the case forward with Birch. What do you think?"

THE MEANING STONES

"Let me have time to think of a way forward. I don't want to frighten Birch off the trail of these murders."

Gammon sat thinking about his next move. He was convinced Gary Birch was arranging these murders but why was the question? He needed answers too. He felt they were being made to look like a serial killer, when they were actually something to do with the gaming industry.

Two days passed, and it was now Friday, the day before the trip to Castleting. Sheba called John just as he was putting his coat on to leave.

"Everything still ok for tomorrow, John?"

"Yes of course, why?"

"Well a little birdie tells me there are a few coming on the bus from the Tow'd Man. One of them is Saron with Sheridan Branch."

"Yes, it's ok Sheba, I know."

"Oh, that's ok then, see you Saturday, John."

"Will do, speak later," and they hung up.

The timing was perfect as DS Yap called.

THE MEANING STONES

"Sir, just had a mate on from Micklock police station. They are raiding Branch's house tonight for illegal drugs, so shall I stand down."

"Yes mate, let them take this on."

John went into see Heather Burns.

"Heather, Micklock police are raiding Sherman Branch's house tonight."

She smiled.

"Yes, I know John, I arranged it. I didn't tell you because the further you are away from his arrest the better for you."

"Well you certainly made my night."

"Can I buy you a drink, Heather?"

"Why not, I hear the Spinning Jenny is good. Jim and Lisa were telling me last night."

"Yes, pretty much my watering hole so let's go there."

They arrived at the Spinning Jenny and Tracey Rodgers was behind the bar.

"Evening John, and who's this?"

"Oh, this is DCI Heather Burns a colleague from the station."

"Pleased to meet you Heather. What can I get you both?"

"I'll have a Pedigree please."

"I think I'll try one of those also."

"A pint?"

THE MEANING STONES

"Yes please, Tracey."

They sat by the fire talking.

"So you were born in Scotland, Heather?"

"Yes, I grew up in Carrbridge, then moved to Inverness when my then husband's work dictated. By then I was Sergeant. We split ten years back. I worked as an Inspector in Organised Crime and Terrorism for four years before spending six years in Major Investigation Team. Then My DCI recommended me for a job down South, and it turned out to be this one, for which I can only apologise for John."

"Don't worry Heather, I have had a love hate relationship with Derbyshire Police Force ever since I came back here."

"So you are not from Derbyshire?"

"Yes, I was brought here but moved to work in Scotland Yard. I was married then we split."

"Are you still friends?"

"We were sort of, but she is no longer with us."

"Oh, sorry to hear that. Here let me get us another drink."

"No way, you are my guest," and John got up grabbed the glasses and headed to the bar.

THE MEANING STONES

"Same again John?"

"Yes please, Tracey."

"I see you are booked on the Castleting trip with Sheba."

"Yeah, are you going?"

"Carl Wilton asked me, so I said yes."

"Oh, that's good then, Tracey," and he headed back to Heather.

"Been meaning to thank you for getting me such fabulous accommodation, and they are such a lovely couple. I was so lucky you getting me that. I won't want to leave John."

Just then John's phone rang.

"Hello, Sir. It's Di Trimble here. I have a man that is really distraught. He said he has found a body with dice for eyes."

"Where is the body, Di?"

"Brichover, Sir."

"Ok, I am on my way back tell him. Have you spoken with Wally and the team?"

"Yes, Wally is on his way and DS Bass and DI Lee are heading there now. Should I call and let DCI Burns know?"

"I'll do that Di, thanks."

Gammon didn't want the team to think he was getting preferential treatment from Heather Burns. Burns said she would go straight to the scene while John headed for Bixton to speak with the person that found the body.

Gammon arrived back, and Trimble said she had put the gentleman in interview room one. Gammon went in, and sitting on the plastic chair with his head resting on the table was a man in his very early thirties.

"DI Gammon Sir, how can I help?"

The man was visibly shaken.

"Sorry, first of all can I take your name and address?"

"Yes, it's Ross Willington. I live at Flat twenty seven, Whitworth Road, Dilley Dale."

"Ok Ross, just take your time and explain what you know."

"I was out doing a run, I like marathon running. It's getting close to Christmas and I don't get a lot of time over that period, so I like to do more than usual coming up to Christmas. I had just come over Robin Hood Stride and I saw what looked like two men in the valley bottom. From what I could see one was sat leaning against one of those Meaning Stones and the other seemed to be looking down at

THE MEANING STONES

him. I thought they guy sat down must have had a heart attack or something, so I shouted, "Are you ok?"

This seemed to spook the guy stood up. By now I am getting closer. He pulled something out of his coat and I realised it was a gun. He pointed and shot at me. I managed to get behind some rocks, but he fired again and again. In all he fired five times. I just hid. To be honest I was shaking, I thought he would come for me. After about five minutes I decided I had to make a run for it. I gingerly raised my head above the rocks and could not see the man with the gun. The other guy was still slumped against the Meaning Stone. I thought I saw movement and thought I couldn't just run away I thought he needed help. When I got to him, he seemed dazed. Then I realised that he had no eyes, just two dices showing a number three and an eye, which I assumed was his eye, on top of the stone."

"Was he still alive?"

"Yes, I tried to help him, but then he went lifeless. I knew, because I was a first aid trainer some years ago, that he had gone. I couldn't feel any pulse."

"Did you see the gunman?"

THE MEANING STONES

"By then I was so engulfed in trying to look after this poor man I wasn't looking. Luckily, I had parked about half a mile away from the scene, so I got to my car and came straight here."

"Why did you not ring from a mobile?"

"I would have done but realised my battery was flat, Mr Gammon."

"Ok Mr Willington, thanks for your help. We will take it from here and I will be in touch."

Gammon set off for Brichover to the scene of the latest grizzly find. He arrived at the small car park, so he could walk along the valley about three hundred yards then up the field to the crime scene.

"Ok lads, what do we have?"

"A male, I would say late fifties. That's all Wally could give us, but he said to say that yes, he will have more for the 9.00am meeting."

"Is DCI Burns still here?"

"No, she left. She said there was nothing she could do, so would see us both at the meeting at 9.00 am."

"Well I guess there is little we can do either until Wally has done his thing. So seeing that we are close, do you too fancy

THE MEANING STONES

a night cap at the Moaning Woman in Brichover?"

"Sorry John, I have to get back."

"That's ok Peter."

DI Lee wasn't a big drinker and rarely stayed out if the lads went for a drink.

"I've got nothing on, if you fancy buying me a beer, Sir?"

"Come on then, Kate."

They entered the seventeenth century coaching inn with its stone walls and flagstone floors all extracted from the nearby Brichover quarry. A tall guy with dark hair and olive skin was behind the bar.

Detective John Gammon Series Three
Book Five

"Welcome to the Moaning Woman, would you like food?"

"Are you Portuguese?"

"Yes I am, Madam."

"How did you guess that, Kate?"

"I have an old friend called Pinto and I could tell the way he spoke English."

"Where is your friend from in Portugal, pretty lady."

"He is from a place North of Lisbon called Marina Grande."

"No, you joke with me, surely not?"

"Why?"

"That is where I was from. What is your friend's name?"

THE MEANING STONES

"Pinto Mauri."

"This is unbelievable, I sat next to Pinto through school. I tell you something, your drinks are on the house and I bring you some of my food to try, thank you," and he kissed the back of Kate's hand.

"Right little charmer that one, Kate." She blushed.

"What a strange coincidence, Sir."

"Call me John, we aren't at work now, Kate."

She blushed again. They ordered drinks and Mario Balluchi, the landlord, who knew Kate's friend could not do enough for them. He brought their drinks over, then he brought some sample dishes of Portuguese cuisine over for them to try.

"What's that John?"

"It says Bacalhau, it tastes like cod fish."

"That's because it is cod fish. I didn't recognise how he had dressed it. They dress them all different ways, John."

They had a couple more dishes and a couple more drinks then thanked Mario as they left.

"You speak with Pinto. You tell him to get here to Brichover and see his friend."

"I will Mario. Goodnight and thank you."

THE MEANING STONES

"Hope to see you both soon," he shouted as they left the quaint little pub.

"Thank you, John, that was a really nice night. Just one question, why is it called the Moaning Woman?"

"Work it out Kate, you are a detective."

She laughed and got in her car. They both drove off.

The following day at the meeting Wally said they had a name.

"Well go on then, Wally."

"Ok, well this man's name is Filigree Columbus Shakespeare Matkin."

"Really?"

"Told you."

"Ok, what else do we know?"

"I know he was HIV positive. He lived at Dalrymple Hall in Ackbourne. He was fifty seven and that's about as much as I can give you."

"Ok DS Bass, let's get digging phone records, bank accounts, police records, anything at all, Kate."

"Will do, Sir."

"So we now have two gay guys dead. Both with the dice an all left by Meaning Stones. Where's the connection, guys?"

THE MEANING STONES

"DS Smarty, you come with me. We best go and tell this guy's friend of his demise."

They arrived in Ackbourne and found the hall. The drive down to it must have been almost half a mile long. Gammon knocked on the door. A young guy who Gammon thought was no older than twenty five or six answered the door. He was very effeminate how he held himself. He was dressed in a ripped tee shirt with tight leather trouser and a belt with studs on it.

"We are looking for Mr Watkin's partner."

"You are looking at him, dude," came the reply.

Gammon showed his warrant card.

"May we come in?"

"Look I don't do drugs, there are none in the house, search me."

"Calm down Mr.."

"Donald, Barry Donald."

"So you are the partner of Mr Watkin?"

"Yes, we are getting married at Christmas. He just has something to sort in London, then hopefully Christmas Eve. Won't it be magical?" he said.

THE MEANING STONES

"Look Mr Donald, I'm afraid there won't be a wedding. Mr Watkin was found dead near Brichover today."

"You are wrong, he is in London."

"I wish I was Mr Donald, you will need to formally identify the body."

Suddenly Barry Donald broke down.

"Get some water Dave, for Mr Donald."

He sat shaking and trying to answer Gammon's questions.

"This is unreal, our good friend Bobby was murdered."

"You mean Robert Bloom?"

"Yes, we have our own little community, Mr Gammon," he said crossing his legs.

"Sorry to ask you these questions, but how did you and Mr Watkin meet?"

"I was a rent boy in London until Bardy came into my life."

"Bardy?"

"Oh sorry, it's my pet name for him, you know, Shakespeare the Bard."

"Oh ok, got it now Mr Donald."

"I fell in love with him the first time we were intimate."

Gammon could see Smarty's face thinking too much information here.

THE MEANING STONES

"So what did Mr Watkin make his money at?"

"He never told me, but some of the boys told me to be careful, because he was a criminal on the dark side."

"Dark side?"

"Yes, that's what they say when they have fingers in all pies."

"So did he have a house in London and still work down there."

"Oh no, Mr Gammon, Bobby who was murdered, persuaded him to leave that life behind and come here, which we did."

"Had Mr Watkin got any enemies?"

"Does Wales have coal, Mr Gammon?"

"I take it from that he had plenty."

"Oh yes, but he shielded all that side of things, he was so sweet. Harbey is going to be so upset, Mr Gammon."

"Harbey?"

"Yes, Harbey Clayton. I think they had a business together, they were very close. In fact a lot of people in our community thought I was with Bobby and Bard was with Harbey," and Donald laughed.

"Ok well Mr Donald, we can get a grief councillor over?"

"I will be fine, unless of course he is a like a Chippendale," and he threw his hands in the air.

THE MEANING STONES

"Hardly Mr Donald."

"Would you need a lift to Bixton to identify the body?"

"No, I have a little two seater number that Bard bought me. What time do I have to be there?"

"If you could be there for 11.00am and ask for John Walvin when you get to the front desk. I may need to speak again so if you intend leaving the county please inform me," and Gammon gave him a business card with his contact details.

"Blimey John, he was a bit camp, wasn't he?"

"Thought he wasn't to your taste, mate. Think we should go and have another word with Harbey Clayton, don't you?"

"Oh, yes I do, mate."

They drove to Clayton's place in Swinster. The old dairy was a very pretty building. Gammon knocked on the door. After a few seconds Clayton answered.

"Mr Gammon do come in. I have just got off the phone with a friend of mine. He tells me Watkin has been found murdered?"

"Yes, that's why we are here. I would like to ask you a few questions, Mr Clayton."

THE MEANING STONES

"Please Harbey, call me Harbey."

"Ok Harbey, Mr Donald said you and Mr Watkin had business interests together."

Clayton wasn't expecting that and stumbled his words.

"Well sort of."

"Well you either did, or you didn't Harbey."

"Well we used to move in the same circles."

"What circles might they be Harbey? Prostitution, human trafficking, drugs, gambling, which one Harbey?"

"Look, I don't have to answer these questions without my solicitor present."

"Fine, we will take this meeting down at the station. Get your coat Mr Harbey it's chilly outside."

"Ok Mr Gammon, me and Watkin met in the mid-seventies. He was an outrageous gay man and I guess I wasn't a lot better. But that all changed in the early eighties with the onset of aids. Poor Watkin got HIV in the early nineties. He was very promiscuous even though we all feared aids. He came to see me to tell me the news. Some ten years later he called me again, but this time he said he needed to get away from London."

"Why did he have to leave London?"

Clayton was shaking uncontrollably.

"Spit it out Harbey, we will find out eventually."

"Johnny Guitar Lomax."

"What about Lomax?"

"Only a very close few people knew he was gay. He was feared in the London underworld at the time, and if it got out he was gay then things might have been different."

"Watkin gave HIV to Lomax."

Detective John Gammon Series Three
Book Five

Gammon was shocked. Why hadn't
Wally told him?

"Watkin said Lomax was going to kill
him to make sure he kept his mouth shut,
so he fled London."

"Ok I get all that, but why would he go
back?"

"He told me when Lomax died he would
go and try and explain things."

"Who to?"

"Look Mr Gammon, I have said enough.
Whoever is killing these people certainly
wasn't looking for me, but if I say
anymore then they may well be, and I'm
not taking that risk."

THE MEANING STONES

"Ok Harbey, I have enough to go on for now, but chances are we will be back."

"Goodnight," and Gammon and Smarty left.

"Blimey, did you see how frightened he was. It's like Lomax is reaching out from his grave, John."

"I think he is scared that Little Gary Birch will catch up with him. He now is my best bet for these murders. Just a second Dave, Carl's ringing."

"John, bad news, Katarina Kosh and four girls died in a fire today. They believe it was started on purpose."

"Oh, I'm sorry Carl, I should have listened to you. Tell Scotland Yard any suspicions they have on the perpetrator I want to know."

"Will do Sir."

"That was the girl that we found Harry Salt was sending money to. She told Carl that she was scared Gary Birch would kill her and the girls if she talked. It looks like he was true to his words."

"You know what John, there won't be a shred of evidence linking him to these girls or the arsonist."

"I know, but this guy will make a mistake and when he does I'm waiting."

THE MEANING STONES

"Come on mate buy me a pint, I think we are getting closer. It's Friday night we deserve some free time."

"Where do you want to go?"

"Anywhere Dave. Oh go on then, Spinning Jenny it is."

Dave laughed at John's transparency.

It was quite busy both, Wez and Lindsay were working. Lindsay said they had set a chef on. She had come from the Wop and Take in Trissington. She said her name was Samantha Woody. John had never eaten at the Wop and Take but he had heard good reports. Lindsay seemed over the moon to have poached her for the Spinning Jenny.

Jimmy Lowcee was at the bar.

"I'll get them, John."

"No, you are ok mate."

"Carol told me what you did for Freda, her Mum, that was very generous."

"Look Jimmy, she should not have told you."

"I won't say anything mate."

"I would appreciate that Jimmy and thank you for the beer."

"Looking forward to the Castleting trip tomorrow, mate."

"Oh, you and Carol going."

THE MEANING STONES

"Yeah, I usually go with the lads, but I will have to be good tomorrow with Carol with me."

"You certainly will Jimmy. Do you know Dave Smarty?"

"Yeah, think you interviewed me over that murder case."

He put out his hand to shake Dave's.

"No hard feelings mate, it's your job."

Dave smiled and carried on drinking.

John and Dave called it a night at 10.30pm.

"Have a good weekend, John."

"I will try mate, see you Monday."

He had just got in his house when his phone rang. It was Saron.

"Did you have anything to do with Sheridan's arrest today, John?"

"No, actually I didn't."

"But you knew about it and you never told me?"

"You told me not to contact you remember?"

"That was for your own good."

"Well, he is arrested, and he can't get bail. So looks like I am going on my own tomorrow night. Perhaps we could have a three-some, me you and Sheba?" and she ended the call.

THE MEANING STONES

Whoops thought John, but it did make him smile. He knew now she was jealous. Now he had to decide what to do next. Tomorrow night looked like being a big night for his love life.

CHAPTER SIX

Saturday morning John got up and decided to read a book and relax. Phyllis as usual had made a cracking job of cleaning the cottage, so he had nothing to do. He got three slices of bacon and cut two slices of uncut bread. He spread butter generously, then a bit of brown sauce and lay the crispy bacon slices on the bread. He took his first bite and took a sip of his strong black coffee opening the page of his book Scarab Falls. He felt like he was in heaven with the stove crackling away in the corner and a light amount of snow

THE MEANING STONES

falling outside. This was idyllic he thought to himself. Time passed, and he was engrossed in his book. He had almost finished it and had been reading for almost three and a quarter hours. He decided to have a little walk. He put his wellingtons and his Rab coat on and walked past what had been his family home. The snow was still coming down. His mind raced back to the time him and Adam decided to build an igloo. When it was finished his mum sent their dad out with a pot of tea on a tray and bacon sandwiches. It made him feel sad. But when you lose your family, memories at this time of year do make people feel sad. He consoled himself with that.

John walked for almost an hour before turning back. It was now almost 3.00pm so he showered and shaved and ironed his clothes ready for the big night. It would be make or break he thought. He had carefully wrapped the bracelet that he intended giving to Saron, if Kev could keep Sheba occupied while he gave it her.

Sheba had said she would pick John up for a change. She arrived at spot on 5.00pm and they headed to the Spinning Jenny to meet up with everyone. Sheba went down the steps to the bar and John nipped to the toilet. He turned the corner in the corridor and almost walked into Saron. She had a pale blue suit on in the style of Jackie Onassis, her long blonde hair complementing the look. She was pleasant so that was a plus.

"Hi John, are you looking forward to tonight?"

"Yes, it's always good."

"Yes, the only difference this year I'm on my own, and you have a new girl on your arm," she said and disappeared down the corridor.

John eventually returned to the bar to the equally stunning Sheba with her ice blue eyes, dark hair and pearl white teeth that lit up the room when she did that seductive smile. By 5.15pm almost everybody going to Castleting was in the bar area.

"Blimey John, this trip is getting popular. Where's Saron's new bloke?"

"Apparently he has been arrested on drug offences and other misdemeanours."

"Oh wow, I wondered why she is on her own."

"I see your ex is here."

"Yeah, me and Phil are fine. I had a quick word with him and Linda. There are no hard feelings on my part."

THE MEANING STONES

"You are easy going, Sheba."

"I'm not John, just sensible. You can't change the way your life is mapped out so just get on with it?"

"Ok everybody, if you don't mind drinking up, the bus is waiting."

"Shout up Kev."

"You heard me Jimmy."

"Think you touched him there, Jimmy."

"Nah, he knows I am only joking, Carol."

Between John and Sheba arriving and coming back out to get on the bus they had almost an inch of snow.

"Oh wow, Castleting will be brilliant
this year, Sheba."

"I know Shelly, can't believe another
year has gone. I only said to John this
afternoon how the kids have grown up,
and now it's grandchildren time."

"Not sure about that Shelley, got enough
on with my sheep," and she laughed.

John looked round and Saron was sitting
with Maisie Smith. Maisie was in her
seventies and lived in the farm close to
Sheba. She had never missed a trip out to
Castleting. She said last year she had been
going fifty five years.

THE MEANING STONES

Saron caught John's eye and he could see she had devilment on her mind. As they approached the main street of Castleting they could see all the kids dressed in ragamuffin clothes. There were gentlemen in top hats and ladies in finery. They covered the full spectrum in clothes of high society in Dickensian times and the working class also. The street took a sharp left turn and almost immediately a sharp right turn. On what was the main street every shop and house had a decorated Christmas tree. The driver took them to the Coach Park and said they had to be back at 10.30pm because they always dropped Maisie off before returning to Swinster.

As they got off the bus Kev asked John if he still wanted to distract Sheba.

"Yes please mate."

"Ok, when we get to the King Charles pub, which will be our third pub, I will think of something to distract her. Are you sure about this lad?"

"Never been more sure in my life, Kev."

The first pub, The George, had the carol singers outside and a guy playing Christmas songs inside.

"Oh John, this gives me a warm glow every year."

THE MEANING STONES

"I know, Christmas wouldn't be Christmas without a trip to Castleting. Me and my brother were lucky to come every year with Mum and Dad. What about you Sheba?"

"Not every year, you know, with all the farm chores. Mum had really tried to persuade dad to leave the farm, it was just in his blood John."

"I think my Mum was a bit more dominant, old Philip didn't have a choice," and John laughed.

They had a couple in there, then Master of Ceremonies Kev, shouted, "Come on, let's try the Grapes."

The Grapes stood up some steps above the Market place. It had a chequered past. People said it had been cursed by a gypsy man.

"Apparently sometime in the 1800's some Gypsy travellers came to Castleting and frequented the Grapes. The landlord, Edward Smirch, was a bit of a lady's man. The grandfather caught him with his eighteen year old granddaughter round the back of the Grapes. He hit him with his stick and cursed him and the pub. It was said Edward Smirch fell down a mine shaft while out walking his dog some two weeks later. Then his wife died of

THE MEANING STONES

dysentery and his daughter was killed on the main street by a runaway horse and carriage. The curse has played on with each and every landlord being besmirched by bad luck, all put down to the curse by the local folk."

"John, how do you know all this stuff?"

"Just with reading books really, and things seem to stick in my mind."

The steps leading up to the grapes were all decorated. They climbed them then entered the bar. The latest landlord had all Gypsy stories on the wall and loads of coloured jugs and things, like they paint on canal boats. The thinking was if you can't beat them join them, plus the story was good for trade.

They had a couple of drinks in the Grapes, but John caught Saron looking at him every time he turned round. They left the Grapes and Sheba stopped to get some horse-chestnuts. They headed for The King Charles and for John his destiny beckoned.

Kev whispered, "This is it, you will have five minutes tops thanks mate."

They were just about to go in when Kev asked Sheba where did she get the chestnuts?

"Just down there, Kev."

THE MEANING STONES

"Would you mind showing me, I love chestnuts, Sheba?"

"No problem, I'll be five minutes, John."

"Ok."

He hurried into the pub and saw Saron heading for the toilet. He didn't know what made him do it, but he followed her in. Luckily she was on her own. Come in here he gestured, and he shut the disabled cubicle behind him securing the lock.

"What are you doing, John?"

He kissed her passionately. At first she didn't respond, but then did. John was touching her all over and she couldn't keep her hands off him. Luckily Saron came to her senses.

"Go John, this isn't fair on Sheba."

John felt in his pocket.

"When you get home tonight open it. It's your Christmas present."

Saron not knowing what was in the package was beginning to panic in case anybody came in. John left. Again luckily nobody saw him, but by now Kev was getting the drinks.

"Where have you been, John?"

"I had to go to the toilet. I think that bacon sandwich I made myself this morning was off. I had to run to the toilet."

"I can see all your shirt is untucked, are you ok?"

"Oh yeah sorry, it was such a rush to get to the toilet."

As he said it he knew it was a lie. The rush was to get to Saron not some food poisoning excuse.

"You sure John? I mean we can stop here instead of wandering around the village with everyone else."

"No, I feel fine now."

John actually felt good. The response from Saron when he kissed, and they fumbled about like two naughty teenagers on their first date, gave him hope she might want to get back together.

After a couple of drinks they made their way outside. Kev had seen the incident with the shirt untucked and Doreen was quick to comment.

"Are you having to bloody dress him now, Sheba?"

"It's an age thing, Doreen," and they both laughed but Kev knew different.

By now there was a good two inches of snow on the roads and footpaths which made the scene even more magical. In the village square the brass band were handing

THE MEANING STONES

out Christmas carol sheets to everyone that came to listen.

"Come on John, get a sheet this will be fun."

Saron was stood straight across talking to Jimmy and Carol.

John sang, but his mind was wandering. He so wanted to settle with Saron and maybe have a family, and do these sort of things.

"Are you ok John? You are awfully distant."

"Sorry Sheba, I'm fine. Just got a lot on with work, you know these killings are taking their toll on me and my team."

"I bet John. They say bookings for accommodation are down fifty eight percent this year against last year."

"I know, but we are working so hard."

"Oh John, I know. I wasn't being critical, it's a good job the Peak District has you."

With the evening finished they headed back to the coach the bus driver took them up Winslet Pass, another area that John was telling Sheba had a dark history. Just then Doreen came up.

"Maisie isn't feeling too well, Sheba. I don't know if you want to sit with her. Do you mind, John?"

THE MEANING STONES

"Of course not."

Sheba left John looking out of the window at what was now a heavy fall of snow. He felt his phone vibrate. It was a text from Saron.

'Are you going home with Sheba?'

He texted back that wasn't the plan.

'Ok let's wait and see,' she said.

They arrived at Maisie's home and Sheba came up to John.

"I think I should stay with her tonight, John."

"No problem, thank you for a lovely evening."

"No, thank you John, it's been lovely. How will you get home?"

"Oh, I'll get a taxi, Broadwalk Private Hire will pick me up. I know Simon quite well, Sheba."

"Ok, long as you are ok."

"I will call you, thanks again," and she headed down the bus with Maisie.

Saron saw her chance and texted John.

'Need a lift big boy?'

He wasn't missing this chance.

'Yes please.'

They arrived at the Spinning Jenny and Kev asked John if he wanted to stop at his and Doreen's place.

THE MEANING STONES

"I'm ok mate, got a lift thanks."

"You bugger, I never known anyone so jammy," and he laughed ushering Doreen away before she said anything.

John got in the car with Saron and it was like he was dreaming. Why had her mind changed so dramatically he thought?

"I'm sorry about not telling you about 'idiot brain'."

I don't think you are sorry for what happened though John. She had to really concentrate with the weather.

"Are you staying tonight?"

"What do you think? Because John Gammon asks me to stay, I will follow like the rest of the sheep. No John, I said I would give you a lift."

"I am confused. What was that in the Grapes all about and then the texts?"

"We are here John, just being friendly," and she pecked him on the cheek.

John got out and she drove off into the night, with John totally bemused. He went in the house and poured a large Jameson's and sat thinking about the night he had just had. What was a matter with him and this obsession with Saron? The feelings were quite like the ones he had with Lindsay, his first wife, and that really didn't end

THE MEANING STONES

well. Was it because she hadn't fallen under the Gammon charm?

Feeling totally lost with the situation he headed to bed. He just got in bed and his phone rang. It was Saron. John could tell she had been crying.

"Saron, are you ok?"

"John, I can't accept this bracelet. It's beautiful. I know what the inscription say's and you are correct. I will never find John Gammon in anybody else, but I'm not looking, John."

"Saron, we can work this out."

"You have said that before, but you have a self-destruct button, John."

Detective John Gammon Series Three
Book Five

"I want to settle down, have a family and a normal life John, and you can't give me that, so I can't accept this," and she hung up.

By Sunday morning John's head was everywhere thinking about what Saron had said. He decided to get togged up and have a good walk to try and clear his head. The walk from Hittington was tremendous at this time of year. It had been snowing during the night, so it wasn't going to be easy walking. He decided to head for Pommie. It took him almost two hours before entering the village with its quaint

THE MEANING STONES

stone water dispenser, which had served the village with fresh water for many years. Although defunct it made a nice central piece in the middle of the village.

Pommie was famous for its well dressings and people celebrating each well in the village. As John headed down into Waterdale he see could all the village kids sledging on what was quite a climb to bring him back towards Hittington. As he got closer he could see the sledges were nothing like him Adam and their mates had when they were kids. They were a lot more sophisticated now he thought.

Detective John Gammon Series Three
Book Five

The sun was bright as he reached the top of the climb where a small trig point was situated. Not that John needed it, he knew his way as he headed towards Trissington. He had decided to have Sunday lunch at the Wop and Take. He was shocked to see Saron and her mother having Sunday lunch. John gestured across to them, but thought this was a mistake on his part. He quickly drank his pint and left. So much for a nice Sunday lunch he thought as he climbed up the fields on his way back home.

He arrived back just as Roger Glazeback and his son had arrived to start milking.

THE MEANING STONES

John had a quick word with Roger before going inside, He made himself a bacon sandwich, not quite up to the standard of a Wop and Take Sunday lunch, but beggars can't be choosers.

The following day John was not feeling good about the world. He had to get to grips that the killer had mercilessly killed four people. Gammon called the team together.

"We are heading headlong into Christmas and we have to find the perpetrator of these macabre murders. We have four murders here in the Peak

District. Katrina Kosh, who we spoke to is now dead killed by a fire. My money is on Birch after Kosh spoke to DI Milton."

"Any ideas?"

"Yes, DI Lee."

"Can't we get Birch arrested on some trumped up charge while we build a stronger case? At least that way the murders stop."

"It's a thought DI Lee, but a long shot," retorted DCI Burns.

Just then PC Magic came in and gestured to DCI Burns.

"It looks like your idea won't be necessary DI Lee. A body believed to be

THE MEANING STONES

that of Gary Birch has been found at Cuckoo Dale Reservoir by some sailing enthusiasts."

The room went quiet. Gammon felt disconsolate, he was convinced Birch was the murderer.

"Ok, DI Gammon, DI Smarty and DS Bass come with me."

"John Walvin and his team are at the scene. Everyone else, time for some door knocking. There are quite a few big houses that look towards the reservoir. Let's see if anybody has seen anything, shall we?"

They arrived at Cuckoo Dale Reservoir and each officer spoke with one of the four witnesses. When John had finished, he walked over to Wally.

"Bit gruesome this one John. His stomach has been sliced open. His wallet was stuffed in his stomach, it doesn't look like anything has been taken. He had this piece of cardboard round his neck."

"What does it say, Wally?"

'GARY BIRCH CHEATING MURDEROUS SCUMBAG ROT IN HELL'.

"Let's hope there is something like a fingerprint or DNA on it, Wally."

"He also had both eyes gouged out and replaced with dice showing the number

THE MEANING STONES

two. Also one eye was left on the Meaning Stone."

Gammon was quickly making notes.

"What inscription was on this stone Wally?"

Wally read it out to Gammon.

'The Butterfly dances near the flickering candle enticing you to play.

She promises plenty if you give her one more penny. She whispers each time, follow me my friend it is no crime.

Soon your pockets are lighter the money you had all gone. With your life now in ruins the Butterfly disappears.

Be warned all you who chance for you win not'

"Thanks Wally, let's have the full results for morning."

"Of course, slave driver."

They set off back with DCI Burns.

"This is a strange one, team. Why is Gary Birch number two? I think we all thought Birch was the killer. Now we have nobody other than maybe Harry Salt. Whoever is doing this appears to know the area very well. I don't think these stones are documented anywhere. I walk round this area and didn't know about the five so far."

THE MEANING STONES

"I have just googled it Sir, on my phone."

"There are nine Meaning Stones. There used to be twelve and they date back to 1810 apparently. It says here that people don't really know why they were placed where they were, but each stone meant something to that particular area."

"Right when we get back to the station let's look at this in more depth, and see if we have a link, and what stones are left and where, Kate?"

"Ok Sir."

Detective John Gammon Series Three
Book Five

They arrived back at the station. DS Bass came through to Gammon with a list of the stones as yet not used.

"Here Sir, this is the list."

"Victim One: Magpie Mine near Shealdon

Victim Two: Truffles Farm near Shealdon

Victim Three: A field a quarter of a mile out of Pommie

Victim Four: A field near Brichover

Victim Five: At Cuckoo Dale Reservoir

These are the four surviving stones left, Sir.

One: Hall Dale Wood, Toad Holes

THE MEANING STONES

Two: Revolution Gate, Winksworth

Three: Annie's Field, Puddle Dale

Four: Buzzard Field, Clough Dale."

"Ok Kate, great. Get DI Milton and visit each stone. I want a report on what each stone says, how difficult it is to get to it and are the stones visible from houses or roads? Then tomorrow we will see if we can get a connection. Either the dice are the connection, or the stones, but I don't see both."

"Ok Sir, I will get DI Milton and we can get sorted."

It was almost 7.15pm when Gammon left the station. DCI Burns had made a remark about his paperwork. Normally it wouldn't have bothered him, but Heather Burns seemed like she was somebody he could work with. So he knuckled down and cleared his desk before leaving for the evening.

John was thinking about Saron. Nothing new there, but should he call or leave her a while? Just as he was contemplating what to do, he got a call from Sheba.

"Hey John, sorry about the other night. Did you get home ok?"

John knew the next question.

"Who took you home?"

He really hated lying.

THE MEANING STONES

"I got a taxi."

"You were lucky with the weather that anybody would come out."

"Yes," he replied. "How's Maisie?"

"She is ok. I stayed with her. They have changed her medication and I think that knocked her up. Reason I rang, I was wondering what you were doing at Christmas? I know it's a few weeks away."

"Not sure yet Sheba, had that much on at work."

"Well, have a think about it, but I will cook us Christmas lunch if you want to.

No pressure just let me know the week before, John."

"Ok, I am expecting Fleur, she might be over for a few days."

"She is welcome as well, anyway have a think. Night."

"Yes, night Sheba."

This bloody obsession with Saron was slowly taking apart John's life. What man wouldn't want to spend Christmas day with Sheba? He must be nuts he thought.

John rang Kev.

"Hi mate, fancy a beer in the Spinning Jenny? I can pick you up."

THE MEANING STONES

"Sounds good to me, John. Doreen's out with Shelly Etchings at some charity make up party, so I'm only watching telly. How long will you be?"

Kev was a very punctual person, so John knew he couldn't guess.

"Eighteen minutes mate. I'll be outside waiting."

John arrived, and Kev was duly waiting with his big overcoat and leather gloves. It had started snowing again, not heavy but enough for Kev to have snow chains on the soles of his shoes which made John smile.

"Get in Kev," John said leaning over and pushing the door open.

"It's brass monkey weather tonight lad."

They arrived at the Spinning Jenny which had been tastefully decorated ready for Christmas. Wez was just finishing off the tree by the fire.

"Evening gents."

"Hi Wez, two pints of Pedigree please."

"Coming right up."

There was a mix of people in but the run up to Christmas was always a bit quiet with folk saving up for the event.

"So how's it going, Wez?"

THE MEANING STONES

"Loving it Kev, kids have settled in school. Lindsay has started running a night class for Yoga in the village hall, so she is getting to know everyone. I'm playing for Swinster on a Saturday, and Villa beat Derby three nil today. Happy days. I was going to wear my Villa shirt, but Lindsay said I wasn't to, it might upset the locals."

"Very wise I think son."

"You are a Wednesday fan, aren't you Kev?"

"Yes, have been for fifty years, but never over egged it. If we beat a local team it's not good for business."

"What about you, John?"

"I support the famous," he said smiling.
The famous, who's that?"

"The famous Man United of course."

"You still look fit enough to play mate."

"No time Wez, but I did say I would go and watch Rowksly 46 some time."

"We play them this Saturday at Rowksly, John."

"Right, I will make the effort."

"I like Waggy who runs them. They say he was some player in his day."

"Yes, they used to come for sandwiches after their matches in the early day of me and Doreen having the pub. They had such a good side that there could be a hundred people coming with their fans. It just got a bit much, so we had to stop it. I think they went to the Wobbly Man if I'm not mistaken. Good set of lads though, never any trouble."

Bob and Cheryl came in with Steve Condray and his girlfriend Fiona.

"What are you four having?"

"That's good of you, John. Stella for me please."

"Do you think you should have Stella Bob? Last time it made you poorly."

"Stop fussing woman."

"Cheryl?"

"I'll have a medium white wine, please John."

"Steve?"

"Pedigree mate please."

"And your good lady?"

"Could I have a glass of Prosecco please?"

With everyone sorted, next through the door was Steve and India.

This is turning into a session John thought, and he wanted to ask Kev's advice on Saron. He eventually managed to talk to Kev.

"It's like this, John. You really hurt Saron and she is making you suffer. I'm sure if she gets a whiff of you climbing into bed with anyone else, that will be your chance blown, so just think on what you want lad."

What Kev said seemed to make complete sense.

CHAPTER SEVEN

The following morning Gammon arrived at his desk to find a large brown jiffy bag marked for the attention of Detective Inspector John Gammon. Police procedure stated he must get any parcels checked for explosives, or anything that may harm him, or his colleagues. Gammon headed down to the forensic team. Wally's assistant set about checking the bag. Gammon stood talking to Wally when she let out a scream.

"Whatever is a matter, Julie?" Wally inquired.

THE MEANING STONES

"Look, look."

Spread on the table were five eyes.

"Oh dear, let me take over," Wally said.

"It looks like the victims' eyes that the killer has been taking, John."

"Bloody hell Wally, why now? I assumed he was going to kill again to make the final dice to be a one."

"Wally, I want everything checking; the eyes the bag, everything, anything that the killer may have just overlooked."

Gammon went back to the office and told DCI Burns about the parcel.

"He will communicate next, John. That was just a warning, I am sure there is more to come."

Gammon went back to his office and he had a missed call on his phone from Fleur. He called the number back and was pleasantly surprised to hear Fleur answer.

"John, I couldn't let you know but I'm here for a week. I hope you don't mind. I let myself in at yours."

"Mind! I'm over the moon. Look I'll finish at 4.00pm. Think where you would like to eat Fleur, and I will be with you soon."

THE MEANING STONES

Gammon called the squad together to go through the connections.

"Ok team, today we had five eyes delivered in a parcel addressed to me."

Just then the door opened, and Heather Burns came in with a tall guy with a brown corduroy jacket and tweed trousers. He had round glasses on like John Lennon made famous in the seventies.

"Sorry Ma'am, I thought you had gone out."

"You were correct. Let me introduce a good friend of mine, Simon Cocklin. Simon is a professor at Derby University Crime studying the connections between the killer's perceived world where he needs to kill. I would like you all to listen to Simon with an open mind please."

Gammon was thinking what a waste of time, but was prepared to listen out of respect for Heather.

"Ok, well as you heard my name is Simon Cocklin and I lecture all over the country but mainly in Derby. Mr Gammon, what if any are the connections?"

"DS Bass and DI Milton, what did you discover yesterday with the remaining visible stones?"

THE MEANING STONES

DS Bass wasn't going to miss her opportunity to shine in front of DCI Burns.

"Well Sir, the first site we visited was above Toad Holes in Hall Dale wood. It was quite a hike. You could not see the stone from any vantage point. To drag a body there would be difficult, but you certainly would not be disturbed.

"What was inscription on the stone, Kate?"

"It said

'These evil woods are not for you. For you have no power here but they do. Goblins and Monsters do rule this wood. Time to leave and don't come back'."

"Ok Kate, the next one."

Gammon noticed Cocklin busily writing down on his note pad as Kate said about the next stone.

"The Minding Stone is at Revolution Gate at Winksworth. This was very visible. It was on the old Derby coaching road, houses overlooked it and the road was still used."

"Ok Kate, the inscription?"

"That said the following Sir.

'Many men will pass this stone. Many men died here in 1801 simple farmers fighting for their rights to food for their

THE MEANING STONES

families. It's with shame hang you head when you visit this stone'."

"The third stone was at Puddle Dale in a field named Annie's Field. The stone was surrounded by a dry stone wall. It was visible from the road and the road was quite busy when we visited."

"The inscription said.

'Annie Weldon witch of Puddle Dale. Tried for your evil encased forever by this wall. May you rot forever in this field."

"Finally Sir, number four was at Clough Dale in Buzzards Field. Not easily navigated to. No road overlooking, in fact the only property was the Lodge owned by Jim and Lis Tink."

"The inscription on the stone said.

'Rest here a while and watch the Buzzards. If you choose to stay be mindful this is Buzzards field and not yours'."

"Thank you, Kate, well presented and well done, Carl."

Kate Bass walked away feeling ten feet tall. Cocklin came back to the front.

"I have been studying your case for some time, in fact since DCI said she was coming to Derbyshire."

"From what I can see, I think the significance is the dice and the gambling angle. I think the first murder was probably random. Then it was picked up by the media, and the killer could see a way of confusing the information. I also don't think the eyes had relevance until you received them back addressed to you DI Gammon. That is now a worry in my estimation. My feeling is the killer is targeting you as the next victim for some reason."

"This may be where he or she has slipped up. I suggest you look at past cases, anybody that may have been released before these killings started. He or she, or even they, are warning you that you may well be next DI Gammon."

"The person or persons doing this are severely twisted, and I believe everybody that died except for the first victim were murdered for a reason."

DCI Burns stood up.

"Thank you, Simon. Simon as kindly offered to share any knowledge with you all that may help us catch the perpetrators. He will be sharing my office for the next two days between 1.00pm and 4.00pm. Thank you Simon."

They all clapped.

THE MEANING STONES

"Ok DI Lee, I want surveillance cameras at each of the remaining stones."

"Milton and Bass, look at anybody released in the last year who DI Gammon had any involvement in their case. Anybody local who could have a grudge against DI Gammon. We need to take this threat seriously."

"John, I need to talk to you."

Heather Burns waited until everyone had left the room.

"This risk to you is very real, John. Simon is a very capable analyst."

"I have been under threat more than once in my career."

"Yes, I don't doubt that, but don't take unnecessary risks. I know you enjoy walking, but don't do it alone. I suggest we meet again tomorrow at 9.00am and let's see what the team can dig up. This Harry Salt character appears to be our only suspect now Birch is dead. It seems too convenient to me the guy lives near the murders. He was tied up with an escort and he works for the gaming commission. I think whoever is doing this is leading us down a path, John."

"I agree, but we have nothing else. Whoever is doing this has it meticulously planned."

THE MEANING STONES

"I just want you to be careful."

Gammon smiled as he left Heather. It was almost 4.00pm and John mentioned he had to leave early to DCI Burns.

John was quite excited to see Fleur as it was getting to the point where he hardly saw her these days. As he turned into the yard he could see a light blue Fiat 500C parked in one of his two allocated parking spaces. John tried his front door. It was open. Fleur came running to him.

"Brother, it is so lovely to see you," she said in her French accent.

"Wow, you are looking well. How come you are here?"

"I can't tell you John, but hopefully I have four days to spend with you. Could you get anytime off?"

"I'm not sure Fleur, let me call DCI Burns."

Heather Burns said she wouldn't mind John taking the second two days of his sister's visit, but with things hotting up she could do with him for the next two days. John thought that was fair enough with it being such short notice.

"Ok John, a friend of mine went to Chatsworth last week. Could we do that one day that you are off?"

THE MEANING STONES

"Of course Fleur, it's beautiful at this time of year."

"Let me get a shower and get changed then we can go for a meal. Where would you like, Fleur?"

"I saw this in one of your Derbyshire Magazines, John. Churchtown Manor."

"Never been Fleur, but it has excellent reviews. We will go there. I'll book a table now."

Before John had his shower he rang the Manor and booked their table for 6.30pm that night.

Churchtown Manor was on the outskirts of Dilley Dale it was run by Christina

Henshow and her Husband Andre. Christina's family had owned the imposing manor for four generations. When she married Andre Henshow, a French chef, the plan was always to open the manor as a hotel and restaurant. It had achieved three Michelin stars in the four years it had been opened. John drove into Dilley Dale, past the old church and now disused junior school. Passing the old gatehouse they turned left down a drive way. They could see the Manor house with the trees decorated and covered in snow like cotton wool strategically placed on the laden branches.

THE MEANING STONES

They were instructed to leave the car at the door and it would be valet parked. John smiled at this as Fleur said she would drive in her little Fiat 500C hire car. Behind them were a Porsche and a Mercedes.

They were shown into what must have been the library years ago, given menus and asked for their drink order. They went for a 1964 red Chianti.

"So John, how are you?"

"Good Fleur."

"You know I'm going to ask you about the altercation with Sheridan Branch."

"Oh, it was nothing. Saron had started seeing him and I was jealous, I guess. He said something about being a plod and I lost it, totally unprofessional I know."

"Well yes, it was. What you didn't know was we have been watching him for almost three years. What I will tell you now is between us."

"Of course, Fleur."

"Sheridan's grandfather started the business, then his father took over, and it was successful. Successful until Sheridan found a penchant for cocaine. That is the reason he didn't want to press charges with you. He knows the force would have

THE MEANING STONES

closed ranks and things would have come out. I couldn't tell you any of this, instead I got him arrested earlier than I wanted."

"I'm sorry Fleur, you must think I am a waste of space."

She looked puzzled at John.

"Waste of space?"

"Sorry, it's just a figure of speech meaning I am useless."

"John, I really don't think that."

"Anyway with Sheridan Branch in prison the real targets are surfacing. Brian Lund's grandson Chico Lund has kept a very low profile, but about a year ago we managed to wire the Drovers Arms and he was overheard talking about a shipment of Latvian girls that he was bringing over. He also mentioned flooding Derby with heroin from Columbia and Mexico. They are mixing it with other drugs that make it more addictive, John. Brian Lund was a bad man, but his grandson is taking things to a different level."

"The other main player is a guy from London, Graham Speers. He came through the ranks and really hit the big time with the death of Johnny Guitar Lomax. Although Lomax wasn't a massive dealer, he had hands in many pies, which Speers saw his opportunity. So we have two, how

THE MEANING STONES

you say, nutcases about to change the social scene of Derby."

Just then the waiter came.

"What would you like to order?"

"I'll have the duck terrine and Melba toast to start, then the red cabbage and spring onion croquettes on a bed of wild rice with fillet mignion please."

"For you, Sir?"

"I'll have the camembert filo parcels, and the sea bass with lime drizzle and dauphinoise potatoes please."

The waiter showed them into the grand dining room. There were about sixteen tables, all finely dressed with white table cloths and King cutlery. John looked up. That ceiling was painted as a copy of the Sistine Chapel that Michelangelo painted.

"John, wow that is fabulous."

"Fleur, do you like art?"

"Yes, I studied Nicolas Poussin at Ecole Nationale Superieure des Beaux-Arts. I love his style of painting."

John sat in awe of his sister, there was so much he didn't know about her.

"That is so interesting Fleur. Tell me how did you go from painting to the job you do?"

THE MEANING STONES

"Life is a canvas," she said in her broken English, "and we build a picture. I was recruited by my government first."

"Which is?"

"I'm sorry John, I can't tell you. This is why I am single. If I have a boyfriend, they would dig and dig. The poor boy would have to be so squeaky clean. I think you say, it's really not worth the hassle."

"You must love your job."

"I do. It has its drawbacks like any job, but I love the action and the danger, John."

"Well you certainly get that."

With the meal finished they shared a Churchtown Cheese board. As cheese boards come out there was more than enough for two from one serving.

The following morning John left for work feeling quite contented. His only family was here, and he now knew more about Fleur than before.

Gammon arrived at Bixton station. PC Magic was stressed. Bixton had played local rivals Micklock at football the previous night, and the uniform lads had arrested four Bixton lads and four Micklock lads for a punch up in a local pub in the town.

THE MEANING STONES

"Look at all this paperwork I have to do, Sir."

"Keep's you in a job, Magic," and he laughed as he climbed the stairs. DCI Burns was on two days holiday looking for houses. She had told John so he arranged to see DS Bass and DI Milton, to see what they had managed to dig up on any releases from prison of cases Gammon had been involved in.

DS Bass said she had located three prisoners who had been released and who Gammon had been involved with. Peter Gambon, but he now lived in the Isle of Man. She had checked with his parole officer who could verify that he was on the Isle of Man. DS Bass he said Victor Nicholl had been put away for armed robbery and assault. Nicholl was a known underworld associate of Gary Birch and had been freed for some years. Now he still lived in Bermondsey, and had a job at a DIY store cutting wood for customers. The manager said he was an excellent employee. Although he had only been his boss for the last eight months, he said there had been no problems."

"The third one was one of Brian Lund's henchmen, Terry Northwood. Northwood was arrested for numerous things including rape, attempted murder and a gambling scam."

"You say I was involved in his case?"

"Nineteen years ago you would have known him as Mick Jonah."

"Really Jonah, that's a blast from the past."

"Well he changed his name while he was in Parkhurst."

"Why?"

"There is no given reason, John."

"Although my name was on the arrest sheet as one of the officers, it wasn't my case. It was DCI Sammy Durward's and he is now retired. So what is the involvement with Brian Lund?"

"Well they let Northwood out after eight years, and it's believed he ran Stoke on Trent for Brian Lund. By all accounts a nasty bit of work, but he has learnt how to let others do his dirty work."

"Right, let's get Northwood in for questioning, and I want Sheridan Branch questioned."

"DI Milton you best do that with DS Bass. He is on remand in Leicester prison."

"Tell DI Smarty to sort Northwood, and tell me when we are expecting him."

THE MEANING STONES

"What about Harry Salt?"

"Let's give him some rope and see how things go for now."

John left work at 4.30 pm to get back and spend as much times as he could with Fleur. On arrival back at the farm there was no sign of the pale blue Fiat 500C. John didn't think much of it he went inside the cottage and made a coffee.

There was no sign of Fleur. Not again he thought. She had disappeared into thin air again, which she usually did. It got to 7.00pm. John had tried ringing her but as usual the phone was dead. He assumed she had gone to work and would ring him the next day to apologise or something.

John called Ackbourne Chinese and ordered a Singapore Chow Mein with special fried rice, and settled down with his book, pouring himself a large Jameson's. He loved Fleur, but she was so frustrating, one minute she was here, the next gone again. He knew her job insisted in the secrecy, but all the same it didn't help with him getting to know her.

The Chinese arrived and John paid the guy. By 9.30pm he was feeling full and tired, so called it a night.

THE MEANING STONES

The following morning it had snowed yet again. Roger Glazeback was already at the farm.

"Hi Roger."

"Morning John, cold one again."

"Yes mate."

"Usual fun and games this time of year with pipes freezing up. My lad is just freeing the water up now."

"Are none of the holiday cottages rented out for Christmas, John?"

"No mate, it's very slow in the Peak District this year. These murders have put folk off, so I am being told."

"Pressures on then for you to find the killer."

"Sure is Roger."

"Oh, meant to say about that young lady that was staying at yours in that little Fiat 500C. Her boyfriend was driving a bit erratic when they left yesterday. Almost knocked me and Snoopy my sheepdog down."

"Oh, sorry Roger, I will have a word."

"No big deal John, just thought I would mention it."

John left Roger and set off for work. Who was the guy with Fleur? He assumed

THE MEANING STONES

it was a work colleague. Flippin' Fleur's whole life story is a mystery John thought.

He arrived at Bixton and Smarty met him to say Northwood and his solicitor would be there in ten minutes. Gammon grabbed a cup of coffee and headed down to interview room one. Smarty had instructed PC Magic to show Northwood and his solicitor to the room when they arrived.

Eventually PC Magic entered the room with Northwood and his solicitor. Smarty started the tape.

"Interview with DI Gammon, DS Smarty, Trevor Northwood and Guy

Manning of Manning and Robertson solicitors."

"Good morning, Mr Northwood."

"Bloody hell, never thought I would be sat across from John Gammon. I thought they would have found you out well before now."

Gammon was used to abuse from low life such as Northwood.

"Well Mr Northwood, the last time we met I believe you were calling yourself Mick Jonah. So do I call you Mr Jonah, Mr Northwood, Mick or Terry?"

Northwood laughed showing two rotten teeth at the front of his mouth.

THE MEANING STONES

"You can call me whatever you want copper."

"For the tape I will address Mr Northwood by his now known name, Terry. So Terry when you left prison where did you work."

"No comment."

"Was it a factory, or a bakery perhaps, or would it have been for a known criminal, Mr Brian Lund?"

"No comment," came the reply.

"You see our intelligence inform us that you were by breaking your bail terms by associating with a known criminal, and working for his seedy empire."

Detective John Gammon Series Three
Book Five

Gammon pushed a picture of Northwood that DS Bass had obtained at him and his solicitor.

"Is that you Terry."

"No comment."

"For the tape, Mr Northwood was shown some photographs of himself and former known criminal Brian Lund. So the question is Terry, if you like we can gather further evidence of your association with a known criminal thus breaking your bail terms, and you will be sent back to complete the original jail term, or you could cooperate."

THE MEANING STONES

At this Northwood lost it he started swearing at Gammon and waving his finger at him.

"Mr Lund was right, you are no good scumbag copper, and you will get your comeuppance soon."

"Is that a threat, Terry?"

Northwood's solicitor calmed him down.

"Answer the question, Terry."

"Look Gammon, I did my time and I am a good guy now."

"I think that's up for questioning, Terry. I want you to look at the following dates and tell me where you were between 7.30pm to 6.30am the following day?"

"I don't know, Gammon."

"Do you want me to help you by checking your mobile phone records, bank accounts etc?"

Northwood looked at the first date.

"I was in Stoke on that date, it's my girlfriend's birthday. On that date we went for a meal at Medio's in Hanley."

"DI Smarty make a note of these answers, and get DS Bass to check them out please."

"The second one, I think I was in London."

THE MEANING STONES

"Can anybody validate this?"

"I was with Gary Birch."

"Very convenient Terry, as you know Gary Birch has been murdered."

Northwood's solicitor whispered to Northwood.

"I didn't know that, I am sorry."

You lying git Gammon thought. Northwood gave a name who they could contact to say he was with them on each of the days Gammon had given him to look at.

"Ok Terry, what were you employed by Lund to do in Stoke on Trent?"

"A bit of driving, odd night bouncing at one of his clubs."

"How were you paid?"

Northwood now whispered something to his solicitor.

"Cash in hand, and he supplied a terraced house for me and my girlfriend to live."

"Is this the same house you live with your girlfriend at now?"

"No, we moved."

"So all the time Lund was alive, you were never one of his henchmen? You never killed or threatened anybody?"

"No."

THE MEANING STONES

"You never sold drugs for Lund or ran prostitution rackets?"

"No."

"You had no business interest in human trafficking?"

"No."

"Pretty clean living boy, aren't you Terry?"

"I like to think so."

"Ok, end of interview for now, we may need to speak to you soon. Please don't leave Stoke without informing Bixton police forty eight hours in advance."

Northwood stood up he was a big man and he looked even more menacing with his head shaved, neck tattoo and the obligatory leather coat.

Gammon showed them out.

"Ok Dave, what have we got to look at?"

"I think we should visit the girlfriend now, and let DI Lee and DI Finney follow up on the others with DI Stampfer."

"Ok John, I'll tell them."

THE MEANING STONES

CHAPTER EIGHT

Gammon and Smarty set off for Stoke choosing to take the idyllic country roads. Although the roads had been cleared, the snow was piled high at the side of the road and the trees were laden in snow. The little villages on the Derbyshire Staffordshire border were beautiful. Gammon had walked many times in the area. They drove through Clacker Lane village.

"Who calls a village Clacker Lane, John?"

"Do you know why they called it Clacker Lane?"

"No, but I have a feeling you might know."

Well in the very old days villages had what they called knocker uppers and lights out men. The men who generally put out the street lights, also woke the men up for work every morning. Nathaniel Gumbridge became quite famous in these parts when he set off to wake the men folk up for work. He didn't just shout, he like yodelled, you know like they do in Austria. So by doing this he woke the whole house up. The women called him clacker because that's how they made the yodelling sound by vibrating his clacker."

THE MEANING STONES

"Interesting little quirks up here John, my wife loves it."

"Yes mate, Derbyshire and Staffordshire appear to have their fair share of characters and traditions."

They arrived at the address that Northwood had given.

"Wow John, look at this."

The house stood on its own in about one and a half acres of land, with a big sweeping drive up to it. An old guy was clearing snow as they arrived.

"Excuse me, is this Terry Northwood's residence?"

The old man looked frighten to answer, but instead just pointed to the big house.

Gammon drove up. This was like something out of fantasy land. They rang the door-bell. A petite young foreign girl answered the door. Gammon showed their warrant cards.

"Could we speak with Mr Northwood's girlfriend please?"

"Just a moment," and she scurried off. A woman in her mid-twenties came to the door. She was very pretty and had the body of a lap dancer.

THE MEANING STONES

"Can I help?" she said holding onto the door seductively, making sure DI Smarty got a good look at her ample cleavage.

"Yes, I wondered if we may have a word? May we come in?"

"Yes, come through. Would you like a drink?"

"I'll have a coffee,"

"And tea for me, milk, no sugar," Smarty answered.

She barked the order to the young girl who answered the door first.

"Bring it into the blue room."

"Come with me."

Detective John Gammon Series Three
Book Five

The blue room was lavishly decorated with fine oak furniture, two large leather Chesterfield settees and carpet you sank into.

"I'm Mandy Slaporia, by the way."

Gammon could just detect maybe a Polish or Latvian accent.

"What is this about?"

Gammon showed the date of the first murder that Northwood had said he was with Mandy for her birthday.

"Could you tell me where you were between the hours of 7.30pm and 6.30am on that date?"

THE MEANING STONES

"Just a minute, I have always kept a diary from being a little girl."

She was gone for a few minutes and Gammon thought she had gone to phone Northwood, but to his surprise she reappeared clutching a diary. She flicked through the pages to the date specified by Gammon.

"Yes, right here. It was my birthday and I went back to Poland for a family party."

"Ok Mandy, did you return with Mr Northwood?"

"Oh no, my mother doesn't approve of Terry. Anyway he is always too busy."

"Ok Mandy, that's great. Thanks for your help."

"Anytime handsome," and she purposely lent forward as she got off the settee showing Gammon her ample cleavage.

They got outside.

"Bloody hell, she was hot, John."

"Just a bit, Dave."

"Let's go and try our luck at the restaurant. Just get Magic to send you through a picture of Northwood so we can show it at the restaurant."

They arrived at Medio just as a picture of Northwood came through on Smarty's phone. A little Italian guy met them as they walked in.

"Good evening gentlemen, a table for two or four?"

Gammon showed his warrant card.

"I wonder if you could help me, Mr?"

"Angelo, Angelo Medio."

"I have this picture, and on this date this person in the picture said he was having a birthday meal with his girlfriend here. Could you verify that for me please Angelo?"

"I was working that night. Mr Terry came in the afternoon for a meal, not the night, and he was with a dark haired lady not his usual lady on his arm."

"Ok Angelo, thank you for your help."

"Is Mr Terry ok?"

"Oh yes, there is no problem."

Gammon and Smarty left.

"What now, John?"

"Before we re-arrest him let's tomorrow do full background checks on his mobile and his banking. This guy is tied up in this somewhere. I tell you what, he was arrogant enough not to try and cover his tracks, bloody idiot. By the time we get back to Bixton it's going to be 6.30pm. Are we having a beer on the way back?"

THE MEANING STONES

"Sorry John, French night remember."
Gammon laughed.

"Ok Michelle, haw, haw, haw."

"Sounded bloody Swedish to me, Gammon."

"I thought that was quite a good French accent."

"Think you need lessons, mate."

"Probably right, Dave."

Gammon dropped Smarty off and drove down the back lanes toward Hittington, and decided to drop down to Pritwich to see if Tony and Rita were still there. John walked in and Rita and Tony were sitting in the corner with Cheryl and Bob.

"Are you still working?"

"No mate, we came out last Monday, but I will buy you a pint lad."

"I'll have a Unicorn then mate please."

So John, how are you after that skirmish with that Sheridan Branch?"

"Don't remind me. You know he is now locked up, Rita?"

"Yes, I did hear, best place for him. So how are you and Saron?"

"It's a bit fractious at times to be honest."

"She will come round, us women are always like that, aren't we Tony?"

"Whatever you say my lovely."

THE MEANING STONES

"There you go mate, one Unicorn bitter."

"So who are the new people?"

"Karen and Phil. She is younger than him. Bob will tell you more, he can't keep his eyes off her."

"Where they from?"

"Sheffield, well he is. I think she is from Rotherham."

"Do they seem ok then, Cheryl."

"Yes, they seem quite good. He is doing the cooking, she is more front of house."

"So what you lot got planned for Christmas?"

"Sleep. Me and Jackie have been that busy with Christmas cakes and Yule logs. It's been nuts, John."

"Good to hear the business is doing well. How's Miss Gosylarnee?"

"She is ok. She has been a bit down. Her mum hasn't been too good of late, and it takes a toll on her, with running the business. At this time of year it's mental."

"Feel guilty Cheryl, I have been that busy with this case. I should really go and see her."

"So what about you Bob?"

"Well Lindsay asked me to do a comedy turn at the Spinning Jenny on Christmas

THE MEANING STONES

Eve, and I think Tony Baloney is doing a disco. So we will be up there."

"Guess we might as well go there then, Rita."

"Well as long as you don't hog the mike and start singing, Tony."

"He has got a good voice, Rita."

"Maybe in short bursts, but I hear it all day."

"You love me though sweetheart."

"You yes, singing no," and she laughed.

"How's your mate and his new woman?"

"Who Steve?"

"Yes."

"Oh ok."

"It was a bit of a shock him walking out on Imogen after such a short time, and then to go with Jo's twin sister. I find it all a bit bizarre."

"Well you know Steve, Bob. He has always been a Maverick."

"You can say that again."

John called it a night at 10.40pm. As he climbed in his car he thought what a nice night he had with them all.

John got back to the cottage to find a note pushed through his letterbox. He carefully undid the envelope.

'Mr Detective Smart Arse

THE MEANING STONES

You don't have a clue, do you? Your sister will be murdered the interfering bitch. The dice number one is saved for you. I really can't wait to take your eyes out while you are still alive and the pain of pushing the dice into your eyes will give me great fortitude for finishing off what I started.

You have lorded your position for far too long and you think your flash cars and a woman hanging on your every word puts you above the rest of us. Well it doesn't, and you will soon find out.

Before I go, just so you sleep well, your French sister is in a lot of pain and because she looks like a female version of you it is giving me great pleasure. You will find her soon.

Goodnight'

John felt a cold chill go through him. Who is this maniac and why kill Fleur? Was it just to hurt him? Fleur was very capable of looking after herself, so he must have drugged her. Gammon called DCI Burns and told her about the letter and the threat to him.

"Ok John, perhaps not what you want to hear. Bring the letter in tomorrow. I'm coming in. Get to bed and get some sleep, it could be a long day tomorrow."

THE MEANING STONES

Ok thanks Heather, I suppose you are correct. See you tomorrow."

John hadn't slept well and wanted to get the letter to Wally with the hope that whoever had written it had left their DNA. On his way in he phoned Wally who said he was already at work, and to bring it straight to him. Gammon arrived with the envelope.

"There you go mate, really could do with a result on this."

"I'll do my best John. Give me a couple of hours and let's see what we can find."

Gammon went to his office and could see Heather Burns was in. He tapped on the door.

"Come in John. It doesn't rain, but it pours? I have just spoken to Sir Keith Mellor from the Home office. He said there is grave concern that this will blow up over the Christmas period. News is usually slow at this time of the year, so the media boys are looking for anything. To be honest John I haven't got an answer."

"We need a break, and now it appears he or she has Fleur. I am seriously worried Heather."

THE MEANING STONES

"I have got DS Bass checking Northwood out. As soon as I have that, and hopefully something off Wally then I will get him back in."

"It's fingers crossed time John, it really is."

Gammon left a concerned Heather Burns to return to his office. His usual stance was to looking at Losehill from his window, it seemed to help him think at times like this. After almost an hour of pondering his phone rang.

"Yes, PC Magic."

"Sir, just had a report of a burnt out Fiat 500C. The old lady who called it in said she thought it must have been joy riders. She saw flames coming from the field behind her house."

"Have you got a name?"

"Yes, Mrs Olivia Nesbitt. She lives at Norman Nesbitt Farm, just outside of Shealdon."

"Ok Magic, I'm on my way."

Gammon drove into Shealdon with the Broken Egg pub its focal point. Climbing up the hill he passed the Shealdon village sign, and about four hundred yards further on he saw the old wooden sign which said Norman Nesbitt Farm.

THE MEANING STONES

It didn't look like there had been much activity on the farm for years. Everything was in quite a poor state of repair. He got out of the car and waded through the snow, ice and farm muck before reaching a green door.

Gammon knocked, and he heard a woman shouting, "I'm coming, I'm coming and tha better not be a bloody window salesman."

She opened the door and Gammon showed her his warrant card.

"Are you Mrs Olivia Nesbitt? Did you call Bixton about a burnt out car?"

"I did lad, tha wasted no time coming, did tha? Let me get you a drink of tea."

Gammon didn't like turning her hospitality down, but it wasn't the cleanest place he had been. Mrs Nesbitt must have been in her very late eighties he thought. She shuffled about in a patterned pinafore with her grey hair in a bun and her well-worn slippers.

"There you go lad, put hairs on thee chest that will."

Gammon was sure the spoon could stand up on its own in the tea.

"Does tha take sugar?"

"No I'm fine, Mrs Nesbitt."

THE MEANING STONES

"So explain to me what happened."

"I were getting ready for bed. I always go ta bed at same time, 8.10pm, always did. See my husband Norman were a farmer tha knows, so he had to be up early every morning. Anyway I went to close curtains, tha knows, before I got undressed and I see this man, and I think a woman, running away from that car on fire."

"Did the woman look distressed?"

"I couldn't tell, my eyes aren't what they were, Mr Gammon. Will I be on tha crime watch program. I like that program. That ginger haired man reminds me of my Norman. We never had a cross word in fifty two years of wedlock. Only trouble Norman had, was he never got over his dad who was also called Norman. He left farm to fight in Great War, but never came back. It affected Norman and I reckon that's why we couldn't have kids. He used to say it's an evil world."

As much as she was a lovely lady, it wasn't helping to find Fleur, so he thanked her and left.

Gammon rang DCI Burns and asked her for some bodies on the ground. Wherever Fleur was being held it had to be within a few miles of this farm.

THE MEANING STONES

"I need to put you through to DI Finney, he wants to speak with you."

"Hello Sir, just took a call from DI Stampfer. He is at Haunting Falls near Monkdale. He was on holiday today, but he has found another Minding Stone."

"What does it say on it?"

"He said it's big and very overgrown. He is cleaning it off and said he will come to the station with the words."

"Ok, I am on my way back now."

Gammon arrived back to be met by DI Tom Stampfer in his walking gear.

"Thanks for coming in with the info, Tom."

"Sir, I know time is of the essence with all this. I can walk anytime."

"Right read it out, Tom."

'Cold and lonely darkness everywhere, just my rifle to keep me company. Blighty seems so far away. The Grave they will dig for me I answered the calling. It's raining. I've waited for hours nobody is coming for me, just my maker. They can't let me die here. We are not brave, we are foolish because I'm scared. If this note is found with me take me home and place me at peace at Haunting Falls in my Peak District. Please do that one thing for me'.

THE MEANING STONES

"I was lucky Sir, I saw an old lady walking in Monkdale. I asked if she knew who the Minding Stone at Haunting Falls was for. She said legend has it that it was Corporal Tommy Crowe. He never came back from the First World War. It's not cared for because it was bought and placed there by Harry Salt's wife. Rumour has it she had been having an affair with Crowe, and that is where they met. She became a recluse, so the stone was never cared for, and I think eventually forgotten about."

"Bloody hell another path leading to the Salt family. Ok tomorrow we bring in Harry Salt for questioning."

Detective John Gammon Series Three
Book Five

It was 5.10pm and Gammon was about to leave for the night mindful somewhere his sister was being held by this maniac. He said goodnight and wondered if he should call Saron? But with everything going on he felt he wouldn't be very good company. The lights in the car park rarely worked, and John had got sick of asking for them to be repaired when he was DCI so gave up. It was quite slippery underfoot, but quite nice evening although cold. Dave Smarty was getting in his car and shouted goodnight when John noticed something on his windscreen. It was a note with what looked like a piece of luncheon meat stuck on it.

John walked back to the station, so he could see what it was. To his horror it was a tongue sellotaped to the note. John read the note.

'Gammon, this little French bitch won't talk anymore. It's time she paid like you will pay. I will be in touch'.

John brushed past DCI Burns.

"John are you ok?"

"Is Wally still here, Magic?"

"Yes Sir."

"Get me all the close circuit footage. I will be back in a minute."

Burns followed Gammon to see Wally.

"What have you got?"

"A note from the killer, and I think he has cut out my sister's tongue out."

"Oh John no!"

"Wally, I want you to look at this. Tell me if this is female and it needs checking thoroughly."

"Can't tonight John, it's the grandkids carol service."

"Please Wally, I'm begging you, help me with this."

Wally had known John a long time and never seen him this distressed.

"Ok mate, it will take me an hour or so."

THE MEANING STONES

"I'll be in my office."

Burns followed the agitated Gammon to his office.

"Look John, this isn't easy, but I was informed this afternoon that Fleur Dubois is a black-ops operative. She works with MI5, MI6, CIA, FBI and the Israel Government. I have been told to back off and that they will handle this."

"She is my sister, Heather."

"I know that John, but I am not allowed to give you resources. What I will say is if you use the resource, then I will turn a blind eye. That's the best I can do. Michael Nolan from MI5 and Hayley

Strong from MI6 will be here tomorrow at 9.45am."

Almost an hour had passed when Wally came in. It's certainly a human tongue, and quite possibly female John I'm afraid. I detected aftershave on the letter. By chance it's the same one I had bought for me at Christmas, called Sensual Fig by Chanel. I also found traces of green lead paint. This is unusual because of the high lead content. The last time I saw this was from the killings at the Drovers Arms in Derby all those years ago."

"Thank you, Wally, I really appreciate your help."

THE MEANING STONES

Wally left in a hurry to get to his Carol Service. He had felt a bit bad about mentioning the killings at the Drovers Arms. He knew that was still quite raw with John with Adam being involved.

Gammon left for the night feeling he had to go to the Drovers Arms in Derby. He arrived at 9.10pm and sat across the street. Things hadn't changed much. The street girls were in and out, often followed by burly minders. John was hoping to see Chico Lund, and it was his lucky night. John had checked a picture of Lund and his associate from London, Graham Speer.

A grey Chrysler 300C pulled up. Out got Chico Lund and Graham Speer. John's attention was on these two, and he hadn't notice two kids on BMX bikes put two petrol bombs under his car. By the time he saw the kids riding off into the distance the back of his car was awash with flames. John got out quick because he knew once it hit the petrol tank it would explode. He got a safe distance, and boom the car went up. By now twenty or thirty people were outside the pub clapping and cheering. As much as he was annoyed there was nothing he could do.

THE MEANING STONES

Some wag shouted, "Long live hot fuzz." A reference to the film and the fact they knew he was a copper.

John called Sheba to ask if she could fetch him? She said she would, so he wandered away and told her he would wait at the bus station.

On the way to the bus station John called Derby Police and explained who he was, and what had happened. They said they would sort and get back to him with an incident number for his insurance company.

Sheba arrived.

"Excuse the overalls and cow muck smell John, just finished helping dad milk."

"Hey that's no problem."

John thought she still looked incredibly pretty.

"Thanks for this, Sheba."

"So what happened? How come you are in Derby with no car?"

"Well, obviously don't repeat this."

"I won't John."

"I was staking out the Drovers Arms. It's a known place for the local criminals to frequent. I was that busy seeing what I wanted to see when two kids, who I am

THE MEANING STONES

assuming would have been paid by these criminals, set two petrol bombs under my car. Luckily I got away before it went up."

"Oh gosh John, are you ok?"

"Yeah, I'm fine."

"Well look, let me get back and get cleaned up. You can have a quick drink at mine and I will run you home."

"Are you sure Sheba?"

"Of course I am, not a problem."

They arrived back at Sheba's and she put her pick-up under the lean-to garage attached to the cottage.

"Pour yourself a drink while I get showered. There is whisky, rum, vodka.

Plenty to go at, just got it in for Christmas."

John poured himself a Chivas Regal and sat at the kitchen table. He knew chances of finding Fleur alive were decreasing by the day. Sheba came down in a white fluffy dressing gown with her long dark hair wet and falling over her shoulders.

"Did you pour me one, John?"

"Sorry, what do you want?"

"I'll have the same as you, and don't be shy."

They sat on the settee with the log burner roaring away. They must have talked for hours. John felt comfortable in her company and she must have felt the same as they both commented at the time.

"Do you mind running me back?"

John didn't want to upset Sheba. They both stood up and with her big brown eyes and sensuous lips. She kissed John.

"Stay if you want."

John was taken back at her suggestion, he never expected this. Sheba slipped off her bathrobe to reveal a beautiful porcelain figure. John kissed her all over before they dropped to the floor in front of the log burner and made love. After what seemed like an age she squeezed John.

"I have wanted to do that for so long, John."

"I never got the impression you wanted to be anything other than friends, Sheba. You are a beautiful girl inside and outside, and I guess I have always felt like this about you."

"Come to bed John, and I will run you to work in the morning."

"Ok."

The following day Sheba took John to Bixton.

"Do you want picking up?"

THE MEANING STONES

"No, should be ok. My insurance will cover a hire car, but thank you. What are you doing Saturday night?"

"Nothing John, why?"

"Well wondered if you wanted to go out for a meal or something?"

"Yes, that would be nice. Have you heard about the Grazing Barn at Puddle Dale? It's got a really good reputation. Shall I see if I can book us in for say 8.30pm?

"Ok."

"I will pick you up."

John pecked her on the cheek as he got out of the car just as DI Smarty was walking past, so he waited.

"Blimey John, she looked a beauty."

"Yes, been friends for a long time."

"Who are you kidding? Friends!"

"Honest."

"Sorry mate, I saw that look she gave you."

"Give over."

Gammon told Magic to inform the team he wanted a meeting at 9.30am in the incident room. He was climbing the stairs to his office when an irate DCI Burns collared him.

THE MEANING STONES

"My office, John. What the hell happened last night? I have just had Jeremy Slattery on from MI5 telling me you were staking out The Drovers Arms public house in Derby and you had your car fire bombed."

"Look this is said with the greatest respect, Heather, but what I do in my own time is my business."

"Not if it jeopardises an operation that's taken almost two years and a lot of hard work by MI5."

"What the hell were you thinking?"

"Again with the greatest respect, it isn't your sister that a maniac is holding and cutting body parts from her."

"John, I know this is difficult, but Slattery said they feel Fleur's disappearance may well have something to do with Chico Lund and his henchmen. They said Fleur had been undercover as a human trafficker, and they think they rumbled her. You have to let them do their job, John."

Gammon sat with his head in his hands.

"She is all I have left Heather. The Lund family have taken everything. My brother, my mum and dad and now my sister."

THE MEANING STONES

"I really don't know what to say, but MI5 will get the people responsible for your sister's abduction. She is one of their own."

"Thanks Heather, I guess it's time to trust somebody else for once."

"John, I have taken the unusual step of asking for volunteers for Christmas day. With these murders I want a team here on standby, what do you think?"

"Fully agree with you. Have you had any takers?"

"Yes, DI Finney, DI Stampfer and DS Yap, so that's enough I hope."

"What are your plans over the festive break?"

"Nothing really planned, just praying they find Fleur safe and well."

"Look Lisa and Jim have asked me over to theirs for Christmas dinner. Shall I see if she has a spare place?"

"Thanks for the offer, but I always find somewhere to graze," and he laughed.

"I bet you do, John," she said in a mischievous voice.

At the meeting in the incident room Gammon filled them all in on the letter with the tongue attached, and his experience the night before at the Drovers

THE MEANING STONES

Arms. There was a cold silence in the room. The whole team were feeling for John.

"My sister's abductor is no longer being handled by Bixton police. This is being investigated by MI5 and MI6. Basically, we are to butt out and concentrate on the dice murders."

"DI Lee, have you arranged for Harry Salt to come in?"

"Yes, he will be here at 11.00am with his solicitor."

"Ok thanks, I am sure there is some tie up with Salt," he said pointing at his picture on the suspect board.

"Ok DI Milton, how did you get on with Sheridan Branch?"

"He basically wants to cut a deal."

"What sort of deal?"

"He wants immunity from prosecution and putting in the witness protection program. He then said he would throw Chico Lund under the bus. I told him I couldn't make that call, but would report our conversation to DCI Burns."

"What are your thoughts, Ma'am?"

"I haven't done anything with it yet. We have MI5 and MI6 here at 10.30am and we have to be careful we don't jeopardise their operation."

THE MEANING STONES

"Ok DS Bass, where are we with Northwood?"

"He has given us the slip Sir, he is nowhere to be found."

"My money is on Northwood now. He may be involved in the murders and my sister's abduction."

"Ok DI Milton and DS Bass, you will be in the interview room with me when Harry Salt arrives. Let me know. Show him into interview room two and give me a shout."

"Thank you everybody."

Burns said she would give Gammon a shout when MI5 arrived. He returned to his office and decided to concentrate on the dreaded paperwork as it was beginning to overflow from his in tray.

DCI Burns knocked on his door and asked him to come to her office as Michael Nolan and Hayley Strong were here. John almost went bow legged when he walked in. Hayley Strong had been Hayley Mitcham and had served with John through his training. They had both become officers together."

"Well I never, John Gammon. I thought you were still in London?"

"I thought you had left the force?"

THE MEANING STONES

"Well sort of left it. Working with MI6 isn't your run of the day policing John, but lovely to see you."

"Ok, well Fleur Dubois was initially recruited by MI6, she was an exceptional officer. Sorry, **is** an exceptional officer. So much so that MI5 and the Israel Secret Service recruited her also. Fleur is a totally dedicated officer, but I'm afraid she did have a tendency to go native at times."

"We believe she murdered Brian Lund a few years back, and this may now have come back to haunt her. What we didn't know was that DI John Gammon was her half -brother. What we need John, is what you know."

"All I know is she said she was coming to stay for a week. We didn't discuss her work. Fleur was very professional. She came to see me, then she would disappear, sometimes within a day. So when I came home, and she had gone I was frustrated, but knew she loved her job."

"When I got the letter, it appears they have cut her tongue out and whoever has done this said they are coming for me next. An elderly lady reported her car on fire and saw two people leaving the scene. She couldn't categorically say it was a

THE MEANING STONES

man and woman, but I believe it was. We have had the beat lads combing a five mile area looking for clues, but as yet we have nothing."

"Ok John."

"So you think this Chico Lund maybe the guy who has got her?"

"Let' say we are keeping our options open, DI Gammon," stated Michael Nolan.

"We have been watching Lund and his men for a very long time. Your attendance at the Drovers Arms the other night could have easily scuppered the work we are doing and have done. I must insist you let us take it from here, DI Gammon."

"Ok Mr Nolan, just get her back safe and sound."

"We will do our best."

Gammon was asked to leave the meeting, which he thought was a bit odd, but maybe Burns would fill him in later.

THE MEANING STONES

CHAPTER NINE

Salt had arrived for his interview and Gammon made his way downstairs. DS Bass set the tape running and DI Milton sat with Gammon opposite Harry Salt and his solicitor, Grenville Durban.

"Mr Salt, thank you for attending this interview today."

Salt was about six feet tall and had a dark blue suit with a cream coloured shirt and a blue tie.

"What is this about, DI Gammon?"

"Well as you are aware, there have been several murders in the Peak District. It has been widely reported that the victims' eyes have been removed and replaced with dice."

"Really, I didn't know that."

Gammon could sense he was lying.

Salt was very arrogant. He sat cross legged and used his hands like a French man to get his point across.

"The bodies have also been strategically placed against so called Minding Stones."

"Sorry, you have lost me. What is a Minding Stone?"

"Got you, thought Gammon.

"I am correct in saying you live in Shealdon?"

THE MEANING STONES

"Yes, mainly weekends, the rest of the time I am in London."

"So, did you not hear about where the first body in the killings of these people was found?"

"I heard one had been found at Magpie Mine."

"How far is Magpie Mine to the village you live in, Mr Salt?"

"About one mile I guess, why?"

"When you were a child, did you not play at the mine?"

"Yes, I guess so."

"Ok, wasn't your grandfather also Harry Salt?"

"Yes, I believe he was, and my father also."

"But you don't know about the Minding Stone at Magpie Mine? You played there as a child, and you are named after your father and grandfather?"

Salt was like a rabbit stuck in a car headlights.

"Oh, you mean the commemorative stone at the mine?"

"Sorry, never heard of the term Meaning Stone."

Another lie Gammon thought.

"Ok Mr Salt, so you work for the Gaming Commission in London. I would imagine you meet quite a few dodgy characters in your line of work."

"There are dodgy characters everywhere, Mr Gammon."

"You can say that," Gammon replied.

"Did you know a lady called Katarina Kosh."

Again arrogantly he replied, "No."

"So you definitely don't know this lady?"

"I said no, didn't I?"

It was working, he had rattled Salt.

"So by your bank records Mr Salt, you withdraw on an average four hundred and fifty pounds a week, which we believe you were giving to Katarina Kosh at one hundred and fifty pounds a visit for services rendered."

"You are talking rubbish."

"Are you saying this woman was some kind of call girl?"

"That's exactly what I am saying."

Gammon pushed a picture of Kosh.

"This is a picture of the woman in question. Do you still say you don't know her?"

"Yes, damn you, I don't."

"Mr Salt, do you know a Gary Birch?"

"Only met the guy briefly once."

"What did you believe his job was?"

THE MEANING STONES

"He was right hand man to Mr Lomax, who ran two casinos in London, so I had to periodically visit these casinos."

"But you say you only met Mr Birch once?"

"Yes, I think that's correct."

"Ok, I am now showing the suspect five bodies and the dates they were murdered."

"Can you tell me where you were on these dates, Mr Salt?"

"That one, I was in London on that date."

"So not at home in Shealdon?"

"No I was definitely in London on this date. Looking at these, I was in London for all of them."

"Do you have a witness stating that you were in London."

"Yes but I'm afraid she is married, so I don't wish to compromise her, Mr Gammon."

Sorry if I am going of piste a little, only I really like that ring."

"Thank you, it is a commission, there isn't another one in the world."

"Really, how interesting."

Gammon felt in his folder on some pictures.

THE MEANING STONES

"I showed you this earlier. We have managed to blow up the hand that his round Katarina Kosh's waist, and look what we found."

Gammon showed a picture of an identical ring. Salt now lost his air of arrogance and whispered to his solicitor. He composed himself.

"Sorry Mr Gammon, that was at a party and I didn't know her name."

"But she knew yours, didn't she, Mr Steve Digby?"

Salt now reacted, banging his fist on the table.

"What are you trying to do, set me up? Yes, I knew Katrina and yes, I paid her for her services. Is that a crime?"

"Lying to a police officer is, Mr Salt. You said you knew her; did you mean know her?"

Again Salt was now under pressure.

"She died in a house fire, didn't she Mr Salt? A rather convenient alibi, I don't think."

"Mr Salt, we have here a search warrant for your property and personal goods, such as your car. We will be carrying out that investigation today. I will hold you here at Bixton until we either charge you or

468

THE MEANING STONES

release you. A DNA test will be carried out, and I have a judge's permission to hold you for ninety six hours from now in custody, in connection to this serious crime."

Gammon was quite pleased with Salt. He just needed a result from either the car or the property search. Wally said he would be working the weekend on that, and would possibly have some answers for John on Sunday. Gammon told DCI Burns he would be in Sunday and if anything was found he would call her.

The following day being a Saturday John had decided to go and watch

Detective John Gammon Series Three
Book Five

Swinster FC against Rowksly 46, Waggy's team. He had promised to go and watch but never had the time. With only three days to Christmas, and being told he wasn't to interfere with Fleur's disappearance, he needed something to take it all off his mind.

John arrived at Swinster's ground. He had forgotten that you needed to be a mountain goat to get to the pitch. He could hear Waggy barking orders. He wasn't sure who to support. He liked Waggy, but drank at the Spinning Jenny in Swinster so knew a lot of the Swinster lads. They had played the first half and Rowksly 46 were

THE MEANING STONES

winning two–nil. The second half was a different story. Wez, the landlord from the Spinning Jenny, moved to centre forward and cracked two goals; one after fifty five minutes then one in injury time.

They said they were going back to the Spinning Jenny for a beer and some food. John declined, he was taking Sheba out that night for a meal.

"Listen John, come down to Rowksly over the Christmas period. We have a game Boxing Day, and we are having a bit of a Christmas Party at the Mouse and Carrot in Rowksly. You are more than welcome mate."

"Thanks Waggy, I'll see how I get on with work mate."

"Well, the offer is there."

Waggy trudged off and John could hear him berating the goalkeeper for the last goal scored against them.

John nipped home, showered and changed, and set off for Sheba's place. Sheba was ready and came out. She quite took John's breath away. She had a black coat, cut at the knee, with a black and white dress and black high heels. She jumped in John's hire car which was a Freelander.

THE MEANING STONES

"Ooh, nice car Mr Gammon," she said as she climbed in a long side him whilst kissing him on his cheek.

"Yeah, always liked these. The one I had was originally my mum's so been ready to swap for a while now."

"Beats my pick-up, John."

They arrived at the Grazing Barn in Puddle Dale. It was an actual barn that had been converted. It had a small parking area. They entered the Barn and were met by a pleasant lady in her mid-forties.

"Good evening and welcome to the Grazing Barn. We have seated you at Daisy's Parlour."

John and Sheba were shown to a small open room which previously would have been a milking stable.

"Would you like a drink?"

"What do you want Sheba, wine or something else?"

"Can I have a Gin Fizz please?"

"For you Sir?"

"I'll have a bottle of Peroni please."

"I will leave your menus. Take your time, we aren't busy tonight so there isn't a long wait for food."

"It's that time of year John, people save for Christmas."

THE MEANING STONES

"This is a nice place Sheba, well chosen. I hope the food is good."

"Shelly Etching mentioned they had been and said how good it was, John."

"Ooh, look at that Sheba, chicken stroganoff. I'm having that."

"I think I will have the salmon, John."

They ordered their food, but no starter to leave room for a pudding.

"Blimey Sheba, that was excellent."

"Yes, I think they will do well. They are Derbyshire folk so know what the locals will like, John."

On the way back Sheba said she had to be up at 4.00am to help her dad, so she didn't want John to stop. She did ask him if he wanted to come to her for Christmas dinner. She said she had her mum and dad and her sister, and they sat down to eat at 2.00pm. They couldn't be much later because of milking she said. John accepted her offer. They kissed goodnight and John watched her go inside the house, then drove home.

The following day, as promised, John went into see Wally.

"What you got mate?"

"We found a book on the Peak District Meaning Stones."

THE MEANING STONES

"Oh and this guy said he didn't know what they were!"

"We also found a diary with Gary Birch, Johnny Guitar Lomax and Katarina Kosh all mentioned."

"Great, good work Wally."

Gammon spoke with DCI Burns and she asked John if he thought Salt was the culprit.

"Heather, I'm not sure. If I arrest him and then there is another murder, the press boys will have a field day."

"What if we get a team to watch him twenty four seven for the whole of the

Christmas period, while he will definitely be in Shealdon."

"Ok Heather, that's probably a good idea."

"Ok, I will release him pending further investigation."

Gammon brought Salt up from the cells with his solicitor, who was not too pleased about being asked to attend on a Sunday.

"Mr Salt, I am releasing you pending further investigations but a couple of questions. You had a contact book with Gary Birch, Johnny Guitar Lomax and Katerina Kosh all prominently outlined, so

THE MEANING STONES

clearly these people were important to you?"

Salt said nothing.

"The other thing intriguing me is you said you didn't know what Meaning Stones were. Yet you have a book on them at your home. Anyway that's enough for now, we will be in touch."

Salt left with his solicitor and he looked shocked at Gammon's revelations.

Monday morning Gammon arrived and got the team together.

"Ok everybody, you are not going to like this, but we have no choice. I need a team of officers to stake out Harry Salt's house in Shealdon. This will take place the week we are off for Christmas, including Christmas Day and New Year's Day. First off, any offers?"

DI Finney said he would do Christmas Day. As did Tom Stampfer for that night.

"Hey lads, very good of you. Right, six days left. Yap volunteered to do Boxing Day night and DI Lee the day shift."

"Ok I will do the next two days. Can you do the next two nights, DI Milton?"

"Ok Sir."

"That just leaves three days and nights."

"Put me down for three days, Sir."

THE MEANING STONES

"Thanks, DS Bass."

"Go on then, I'll do the three nights."

"That's great, DI Finney."

"All of you, thanks. We will be staking out Harry Salt's house and recording his every movement. This is where he lives. From Christmas Day, tomorrow at 7.00am, starting with DI Finney until 7.00pm, then DI Stampfer and so on. You all have my mobile number and I would like a full report after each of your shifts. Don't worry about the time, I need to know. To all of you have a great Christmas and thanks for the gesture."

Gammon decided to go straight home with it being Christmas Eve. He washed and showered, and decided to go to the Tow'd Man vainly in the hope of seeing Saron.

The pub was very busy. As he entered the bar area Donna and Saron had made quite an impact with the decorations.

"Hey John, lovely to see you."

"And you Donna, busy night."

"Yeah, we have got Swinster Guisers here at 9.00pm, on their usual tour of the pubs. At 10.00pm we have Dilley Dale Church Choir singing carols round the

THE MEANING STONES

Christmas tree. I do love this time of year, don't you?"

"Yes, special time Donna."

Just then Saron came through in her chef whites.

"Oh hi John, you ok?"

"Yeah, thought I would call and wish you a Happy Christmas."

Saron leaned forward and pecked him on the cheek, and quietly whispered thank you for her bracelet.

That gesture meant so much to John. It was a show of affection from Saron which in his mind made him still in with a chance.

Detective John Gammon Series Three
Book Five

Saron finally came into the bar just has the choir singers started their Christmas Carol singing. She had a blue Christmas jumper with a snowman on the front and tight jean leggings. John wondered how a naff Christmas jumper could look so classy, but it was the girl inside it he thought. Oh how he wished he could turn back the clock. But looking at Saron, she seemed to have moved on, where he was still hankering after her.

"How's Sheba, John?"

"Yeah good, thanks. She has asked me over for Christmas dinner."

Saron's face dropped.

THE MEANING STONES

"Oh, that's nice then," she said through gritted teeth.

Saron knew Sheba was stunning and possibly the biggest competition for her. It got to midnight and Saron was locking up.

"Are you going home, John?"

"Are you asking me to stay?"

"If you want to. I wouldn't want to upset Sheba though."

"Don't be silly, we are mates."

"Ok, well I told Donna to get off. So just finish moving the glasses and lock up, then come up. I'll take a bottle of champagne."

This is turning out better than he had expected John thought. He turned the lights off and headed up-stair to Saron's en-suite bedroom. She was laying on the bed in a black all in one camisole with black stockings and black kitten heel shoes. Her hair she had swept to one side revealing her small right ear which she had always liked John to caress. He took his clothes off and lay beside her. She passed him a glass of champagne. He took two sips then placed his and her glasses on the bedside cabinet. He slowly kissed and caressed Saron from her feet to her ears, stopping at strategic places to give them his full attention. Saron was writhing in ecstasy. She was moaning.

"Make love to me, Gammon."

John concentrated. He wanted this to be a performance above all others, he wanted Saron to want him even more.

The following morning she left John in bed but returned with a mince pie and a Brandy Baileys.

"Wish you were staying here for Christmas Day, John."

"I will feel bad having said I would go to Sheba's."

"I know, I understand. There is me, Donna, and I invited Kev and Doreen. I thought that would have been a nice surprise for you."

"Oh you are making me feel bad now."

"No, don't it's my silly fault."

Saron got dressed, kissed John and said have a nice day as he set off for Sheba's. There had been a dusting of snow during the night and the fields took on a magical display with the snow glistening in the fields. John's heart was heavy though thinking of Fleur, but he knew he just had to trust MI5 and MI6. Sheba s little

THE MEANING STONES

cottage was quite full with presents and quite a large tree for the size of the room.

They all had their Christmas hats on and John was given a pirate's hat to wear.

"What we do John is first we have the presents and a brandy each as we open them."

"So let's start. One for you Julia."

Sheba's sister was a pleasant girl, a bit older than Sheba, but a really good laugh.

"Now you dad, one for mum. Oh, and look at this, one for John."

Everyone seemed mystified. All of them assumed Sheba had bought John something. It was a small box the type

wedding rings come in, nicely decorated
with a brown bow.

"I don't know what to say, thank you,"
and kissed Sheba.

"Enjoyed the kiss John, but I didn't buy
you anything."

Sheba's Mum had gone to the toilet
claiming the brandy was going straight
through her.

"Mum, check the roast potatoes on your
way back."

"Mum must have got you a bit of
something, she would not want you left
out."

THE MEANING STONES

"Well that's very kind of her," he said undoing the little mystery box.

"Blimey, has she bought you a ring? Look out Dad, think Mum's fooling around," and Sheba laughed.

John opened the box and to his horror a human eye was staring at him. Fleur's eyes had slight brown flecks in them. He noticed that from when he first met her. This eye had the same abnormality. John sat cold looking at what he knew was his sister's eye in front of him.

"You ok John?"

"I have to phone Bixton Police."

Detective John Gammon Series Three
Book Five

To be continued...................

Printed in Great Britain
by Amazon